"So, how much did you make off my brother?"

"The money ha said, his voice dan............ in because he wa...............

"You don't shoot friends in the leg. You should have let him go."

"He'd never have gotten away, Aubrey. And if the wrong cop had found him, he'd have been dead." Beau literally had to bite his tongue to keep his temper from boiling over. He knew Aubrey would never believe her precious older brother, half-insane with desperation, had fired the first shot.

"You've already made up your mind about me. I'm the bad guy. Nothing I could say would change your opinion, so why bother?" He suddenly realized he was on his feet.

Her eyes filled with tears as she looked up at him. "Because I don't want you to be the bad guy."

Dear Harlequin Intrigue Reader,

We've got an intoxicating lineup crackling with passion and peril that's guaranteed to lure you to Harlequin Intrigue this month!

Danger and desire abound in *As Darkness Fell*—the first of two installments in Joanna Wayne's HIDDEN PASSIONS: Full Moon Madness companion series. In this stark, seductive tale, a rugged detective will go to extreme lengths to safeguard a feisty reporter who is the object of a killer's obsession. Then temptation and terror go hand in hand in *Lone Rider Bodyguard* when Harper Allen launches her brand-new miniseries, MEN OF THE DOUBLE B RANCH.

Will revenge give way to sweet salvation in *Undercover Avenger* by Rita Herron? Find out in the ongoing NIGHTHAWK ISLAND series. If you're searching high and low for a thrilling romantic suspense tale that will also satisfy your craving for adventure—you'll be positively riveted by *Bounty Hunter Ransom* from Kara Lennox's CODE OF THE COBRA.

Just when you thought it was safe to sleep with the lights off…*Guardian of her Heart* by Linda O. Johnston—the latest offering in our BACHELORS AT LARGE promotion—will send shivers down your spine. And don't let down your guard quite yet. Lisa Childs caps off a month of spine-tingling suspense with a gripping thriller about a madman bent on revenge in *Bridal Reconnaissance*. You won't want to miss this unforgettable debut of our new DEAD BOLT promotion.

Here's hoping these smoldering Harlequin Intrigue novels will inspire some romantic dreams of your own this Valentine's Day!

Enjoy,

Denise O'Sullivan
Senior Editor
Harlequin Intrigue

BOUNTY HUNTER RANSOM
KARA LENNOX

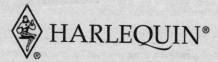

TORONTO • NEW YORK • LONDON
AMSTERDAM • PARIS • SYDNEY • HAMBURG
STOCKHOLM • ATHENS • TOKYO • MILAN • MADRID
PRAGUE • WARSAW • BUDAPEST • AUCKLAND

ISBN 0-373-22756-6

BOUNTY HUNTER RANSOM

Copyright © 2004 by Karen Leabo

This edition published by arrangement with Harlequin Books S.A.

® and TM are trademarks of the publisher. Trademarks indicated with ® are registered in the United States Patent and Trademark Office, the Canadian Trade Marks Office and in other countries.

Visit us at www.eHarlequin.com

Printed in U.S.A.

ABOUT THE AUTHOR

Texas native Kara Lennox has been an art director, typesetter, textbook editor and reporter. She's worked in a boutique, a health club and an ad agency. She's been an antiques dealer and even a blackjack dealer. But no work has made her happier than writing romance novels.

When not writing, Kara indulges in an ever-changing array of weird hobbies. (Her latest passions are treasure hunting and creating mosaics.) She loves to hear from readers. You can visit her Web site and drop her a note at www.karalennox.com.

Books by Kara Lennox

HARLEQUIN INTRIGUE
756—BOUNTY HUNTER RANSOM†

HARLEQUIN AMERICAN ROMANCE
841—VIRGIN PROMISE
856—TWIN EXPECTATIONS
871—TAME AN OLDER MAN
893—BABY BY THE BOOK
917—THE UNLAWFULLY WEDDED PRINCESS
934—VIXEN IN DISGUISE*
942—PLAIN JANE'S PLAN*
951—SASSY CINDERELLA*
974—FORTUNE'S TWINS
991—THE MILLIONAIRE NEXT DOOR

*How To Marry a Hardison
†Code of the Cobra

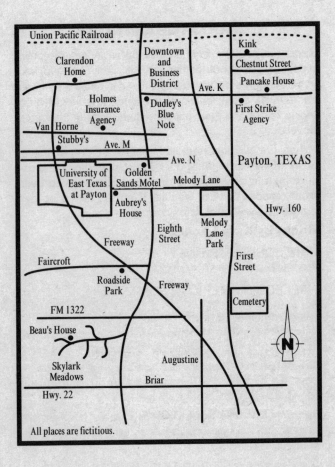

Union Pacific Railroad

Kink

Clarendon Home

Downtown and Business District

Chestnut Street

Pancake House

Ave. K

Holmes Insurance Agency

Dudley's Blue Note

First Strike Agency

Van Horne

Stubby's

Ave. M

Ave. N

Payton, TEXAS

University of East Texas at Payton

Golden Sands Motel

Melody Lane

Aubrey's House

Hwy. 160

Eighth Street

Melody Lane Park

Freeway

First Street

Faircroft

Roadside Park

Freeway

FM 1322

Cemetery

Beau's House

N

Skylark Meadows

Augustine

Briar

Hwy. 22

All places are fictitious.

CAST OF CHARACTERS

Aubrey Schuyler—Even after she is assaulted, the police won't take her fears for her missing cousin seriously. She's forced to turn to childhood friend Beau Maddox—the man who shot her brother and sent him to prison.

Beau Maddox—Ex-cop, bounty hunter, Beau believes he might redeem himself in Aubrey's eyes if he can bring baby Sara home safe.

Patti Clarendon—Aubrey's flighty cousin has a history of drug addiction. So when she disappears with her baby, Aubrey knows she's in trouble.

Sara Clarendon—Patti's six-month-old daughter.

David Clarendon—Aubrey's cousin vows to move heaven and earth to bring his sister and niece home unharmed.

Wayne Clarendon—Aubrey's millionaire uncle is dying of cancer. But he's not so ill that he can't offer a million-dollar reward for the granddaughter he's seen only once.

Lyle Palmer—The incompetent detective sees this case as his chance to get his name in the paper.

Greg Holmes—The crooked insurance agent is Patti's boss, and it's rumored they were having an affair. How far would he go to protect his secrets?

Summer Deetz—She works with Patti at the insurance agency, and she sure acts as if she's got something to hide.

Cory Silvan—Bartender at the alternative nightclub where Patti moonlights, he is also Patti's drug dealer.

Charlie Soffit—Baby Sara's father is a rough-looking, hard-drinking biker with whom Patti had a rocky relationship.

Chapter One

"Just please hurry home. I need you real bad."

Aubrey Schuyler stared at her cell phone. What now? Ever since her cousin Patti had come to live with Aubrey, life had been full of surprises, most of them unpleasant. But today was worse than usual. The phone call had interrupted a faculty meeting, and Patti's voice had sounded desperate.

Aubrey dared not ignore her cousin's summons, not when a little baby was involved. Patti tried to be a good mother to six-month-old Sara, but, bless her heart, she had the common sense God gave a squirrel.

As Aubrey pulled up to her sturdy, prairie-style home, she noted that Patti's battered Escort wasn't in the driveway. Why on earth would her cousin call Aubrey home, then leave before she arrived? Had the car been stolen? Was that the big crisis?

Aubrey's bare legs stuck to the vinyl seat as she exited her Jeep Wrangler, and the back of her pale blue T-shirt was damp. She pulled her heavy mass of curly auburn hair off her neck for a few moments, hoping in vain for a slight breeze. But there was none. She dropped her hair, grabbed her keys and headed resolutely for the front door.

It turned out a key wasn't necessary. Patti had left the front door unlocked again, though Aubrey had asked her many times to be more careful. Payton, Texas, wasn't the safe little burg it had been during their childhood. The university where Aubrey taught chemistry had grown quickly over the last decade, and the town's population had exploded.

Aubrey pushed the front door open. "Patti?"

No answer. She headed upstairs and into Patti's bedroom, which was in its usual state of disarray. Drawers were half-open, clothing strewn over the unmade bed.

Aubrey peeked into the nursery. Sara's car seat was gone.

Had Aubrey misunderstood the call? As she pondered the puzzle a crawling sensation wiggled up her spine. Something was wrong. Was it an item out of place? A strange odor in the air?

She scarcely had time to think about getting out of the house when the closet door behind her burst open and someone grabbed her with an arm around the neck. She screamed and kicked as panic took over. But her assailant was strong, abetted by his own burst of adrenaline. The arm wedged around her neck was hard and unyielding. She kicked backward, but her attacker avoided the worst of her blows, not that her sneakers would do much damage anyway. His other arm was wrapped around her body, pinning her arms to her sides. He was not a large man, but he knew how to fight. He smelled of unwashed male.

The man was trying to drag her out of the nursery— but to where? Aubrey thought frantically back to a self-defense course she'd taken at the University years ago. *Use whatever you have at hand as a weapon. Keys, fingernails, teeth.*

That was it. Counting on the element of surprise, Aubrey struck like a snake, clamping her mouth down hard on the man's forearm, the only part of his anatomy she could reach. She tasted sweat and blood. He rewarded her with a grunt of pain, and his hold on her loosened fractionally. She bent her knees and tried to slide downward, at the same time pushing him off balance.

For a brief, exultant moment, she thought she was going to escape. She lunged for the door just as something whacked her on the head. The first blow merely stunned her. She started to turn so she would ward off the next blow, but she was too slow. The next slam to her head knocked her down, and she was out.

When next Aubrey opened her eyes, she knew some time had passed, but not how much. Her head pounded and her stomach roiled with nausea. She was still on the floor of the nursery. She reached for her face and found it covered with sticky blood.

Oh, God, was she badly hurt? Was he still here? She listened, but all was quiet.

It seemed to take forever for her to sit up and get her bearings. She wasn't seriously injured, at least she didn't think so. Just a bump on the head and a lot of blood. A broken lamp on the floor appeared to be her attacker's weapon. The phone. She needed to call the cops. Where were Patti and Sara? Had they fled from danger, or had some more sinister fate befallen them?

Aubrey pulled herself to her feet and walked unsteadily to her own bedroom. It was trashed. Her jewelry box was empty, her portable TV gone.

And her phone. The bastard had stolen her cordless phone.

Outrage gave her strength. She turned and headed

down the hall, down the stairs, still a little dizzy but better with each step. He couldn't steal the old-fashioned wall phone from the kitchen. She grabbed the receiver and dialed 911. After reporting the incident as calmly and clearly as she could, she stumbled to the sink and threw up. She rinsed her mouth, washed the blood off her face. She probed her scalp and found the source of the blood, a goose egg swelling with a small cut. It felt as if the cut had stopped bleeding, so she went to sit on her front porch and wait for the police. Her older brother, Gavin, had been a cop, and she knew enough to not further pollute the crime scene.

She'd hardly sat down when she heard the low rumble of a car engine approaching. She thought it was the police, until the vehicle pulled into view. It was a souped-up black Mustang convertible, and the dark-haired driver didn't appear the least bit coplike.

When the car pulled into her driveway she jumped to her feet, heart pounding, and wondered whether to find a weapon or dart inside and lock the door. Then something about the man behind the wheel tugged at her memory. The shape of his broad shoulders, the way he gripped the steering wheel…

She froze, her hand on the doorknob as the man got out of the car and she realized who it was. She relaxed only a fraction. Beau Maddox. What the hell was that son of a bitch doing here?

Her palms went damp and her mouth felt full of cotton as he headed toward her, his motorcycle boots crunching against the gravel. Even as her fury rose, another emotion battled it. The sight of his tall, muscular frame had once made her adolescent heart flutter with anticipation. The hard lines of his face, the eyes like chips of ice, the charcoal hair he was forever pushing out of his face, the gesture remaining even when he cut his hair short for the police academy. All of those things had been burned into her brain with the branding iron of young love.

Well, she didn't love him now, she reminded herself. She hated him. And her silly physiological reactions were nothing but memory, a bunch of misguided chemicals racing around in her body looking for a neuro-receptor to grab on to.

Her hand dropped from the doorknob and she turned to face him. "What are you doing here?"

"Damn, Aubrey, are you all right? I heard the call go out on the police scanner—"

"I'm fine." But she wasn't fine. She was shaken to her center, barely holding on to calm. Her home had been invaded, her security shattered, her cousin and precious baby Sara missing. She could have died. Maybe her attacker had meant to kill her. He could have fractured her skull.

Beau took a step toward her and grabbed her arm. She would have shaken loose, indignant, until she realized Beau was all that kept her from crumpling to the ground.

He guided her to a battered wicker chair on the front porch. "Sit down before you fall down. What the hell happened? Where are you hurt?" He began probing her scalp with surprisingly gentle hands, searching for the head wound. She batted his hands away.

"I'm okay. Apparently I interrupted a burglary in progress. The guy bashed me in the head, trashed my house and left. At least, I think he left."

Beau's gaze darted to her front door, and she knew he wanted to go in there and check things out. He'd been a cop for three years. But he'd given up the right to be first at a crime scene when he'd turned in his badge.

"Don't even think about it," she said. "Cops will be here any minute, and you can be on your way."

"I'm not budging. You need to go to the hospital. Were you knocked out?"

Aubrey's memories of the attack were a bit fuzzy, but she didn't think she'd been unconscious for long. "I'm fine."

"Fine, my ass." He pulled a bandana from the back pocket of his black jeans and wiped her face with it. Apparently her wound was still oozing blood. "Don't worry, this is clean. Here, hold it against the cut."

She did as instructed, only because she knew he was right. She needed to stop the bleeding before the cops arrived, or they'd make her go to the hospital for sure.

"Tell me what happened," he insisted. "Did you get a look at the guy?"

"No. He came at me from behind. He was white, and I can make an educated guess about his height, but that's it. Oh, wait a minute." She thought for a moment. "I bit him."

"What?" Beau actually grinned. "You tiger, you."

"Oh, shut up. I did some damage to his right forearm. I remember tasting blood."

Beau grew serious. "You might have some biological evidence in your mouth. We should swab it out right away, before your own saliva washes away the—"

"It's no good. I, um, threw up afterward and rinsed my mouth out."

"Hell."

Aubrey felt a bit calmer now, and she had to admit

she was actually grateful for Beau's presence. Whatever he'd done in the past, he'd never intended to hurt her, and she knew he could protect her better than just about any man alive. He'd been good as a cop, and was even better as a bounty hunter. Unfortunately.

A squad car pulled up and a young, lone patrolman got out. Aubrey quickly told her story. He looked at her and took a quick tour of the house to make sure the perpetrator was really gone, then called for an evidence team, a detective and paramedics.

"I don't need the paramedics," she objected.

"Let them at least look at you," Beau said.

The cop, who'd ignored Beau until now, suddenly focused his attention on him. "Who are you?"

"A friend," Aubrey answered quickly before Beau could smart off. He'd left the force with a lot of bitterness. The whole department, he'd claimed, had been riddled with incompetence and downright corruption. Aubrey's brother had been only a small part of it but Beau's superiors were unwilling to go after the big fish. Beau had quit in protest.

"And where were you when all this happened?" the cop asked.

"He wasn't here," Aubrey said.

"I can answer for myself," Beau said evenly. He handed the cop a card that read First Strike Bounty Hunters. It featured a logo of a coiled snake and the motto, Code of the Cobra.

"Beau Maddox," the cop read aloud. "I know who you are. You're the one who brought in Gavin Schuyler." He glanced down at his notepad, then at Aubrey, then back at Beau. "Schuyler?"

"Gavin's my brother."

"And if you know what's good for you, you'll drop

the subject before she gets started,'' Beau said, as if she were the one who'd done something wrong.

''Okay, that's it.'' She pointed toward the street. ''Go.''

The cop shrugged as if to say, *Women.* ''Better do what she says. She might bite you, too.'' The two men shared a look that infuriated Aubrey further. Men were such jerks sometimes.

An unmarked car pulled into Aubrey's driveway behind the squad car, and a detective with reddish-brown hair got out. He wore a long-sleeved shirt despite the oppressive heat, his tie neatly knotted.

Then she realized she knew him, which wasn't all that surprising. She'd met lots of men and women from the force when she hung out with her brother and his friends, including Beau, once his very best friend. That seemed a lifetime ago.

The detective was Lyle Palmer. He'd been one of the regulars, along with Beau and Gavin, who hung out at Dudley's Blue Note after hours. Dudley's was a cop bar that hadn't changed one square foot of Formica since the fifties. The cops liked the no-frills atmosphere and the cheap, strong drinks.

Aubrey had spent quite a few hours there, too, during grad school, always hoping Beau would finally notice her. Looking back on it, she found her previous crush on him pathetic. She'd brought Patti with her a couple of times, hoping to get her interested in a higher caliber man than she normally dated. Lyle had taken an instant shine to Patti, but she'd rebuffed his flirtation—rather rudely, Aubrey recalled. Later she'd said there was no way she was dating a cop, especially one that reminded her of Howdy Doody.

''Aubrey.'' Lyle treated her to a warm smile.

"When I heard your name, I volunteered—" His gaze flickered to Beau, then fixed on him. "Maddox? Might have known I'd find you in the thick of trouble."

Aubrey recall that the two men hadn't liked each other, but the specifics eluded her.

"When did you make detective?" Beau asked mildly, not rising to the bait.

Lyle puffed up a bit. "Around the first of the year."

"Yeah? Whose ass did you have to lick to get the promotion?"

Lyle's eyes narrowed. "I could make your life miserable, you know."

Aubrey cleared her throat. "This isn't helping."

Lyle returned his attention to her, looking contrite. "Sorry. What the hell happened here?"

So she told her story again, adding little bits as she remembered them, and the patrolman added his two cents before taking off.

"Listen, Lyle, I'm really worried about my cousin Patti. You remember her, right?" She tensed, waiting for a negative reaction. But Lyle remained ultraprofessional.

"Yeah, I remember."

"I was in a meeting when she called me on my cell phone sounding terribly upset. And when I got here, she and the baby were gone, and some guy was in my house."

"But you say her car wasn't here when you arrived home?" Lyle asked.

"That's right."

"Maybe she knew bad news was on the way and she cleared out ahead of it. She's, um, been in a bit of trouble in the past."

Aubrey glanced at Beau, who was still here just to

drive her crazy, she was sure. She pleaded with her eyes for him to keep quiet. "Patti has kept her nose clean for over a year, ever since she found out she was pregnant."

"Is it possible someone from her past has come back to bother her?" Lyle asked, jotting a few notes.

"I suppose. Oh, wait, maybe that's it! There's Charlie Soffit, Sara's father. He's a low-life biker. He kicked her out when Patti told him she was pregnant, but then he keeps coming around to harass her. But he's never been violent. I think…well, Patti's father is rich."

"I know who Patti's father is," Lyle said, which wasn't surprising. Wayne Clarendon was one of Payton's most prominent citizens, a descendant of the town's founder.

"I think Charlie wants a piece of that," Aubrey continued, "and he thinks he can get it by using Sara."

"Does he have any visitation rights?" Beau asked.

Lyle shot him a nasty look. "This isn't your investigation, Maddox."

Beau shrugged, unperturbed. "Someone has to ask the right questions."

"Patti got him to sign away parental rights," Aubrey answered, hoping to distract the two snarling dogs from each other. "But maybe he wishes he hadn't done that."

"Sounds like a suspect to me," Beau said.

Aubrey pointed toward Beau's Mustang. "Leave!"

Beau held up both hands in a gesture of surrender. "Okay, fine. Can't blame a guy for showing a little concern for an old friend."

"Make no mistake, that is *not* what I blame you for."

It suddenly got very quiet, and Aubrey wished she'd kept her mouth shut. But the words were out now. The ones she *hadn't* spoken were especially loud. *I blame you for shooting my brother.*

Beau's gaze narrowed. "I saved Gavin's life. But you'll never understand that because you don't want to. You'd rather hold on to that tunnel vision that lets you believe your precious brother could do no wrong."

Beau turned and stomped off the porch and out to his car. He backed up the Mustang, then drove through her yard as the patrolman had, nearly crashing into the crime scene van as it pulled up.

"You're not really friends with him anymore, are you?" Lyle asked.

She shook her head. "We've hardly talked since he left the force. I don't even know what brought him here today, unless it was morbid curiosity." She mentally shook herself. She had more important things to worry about than the lingering animosity between her and Beau Maddox. "So you'll check out Charlie Soffit?"

"Yeah. It's possible he's involved." Lyle flipped his notebook closed and stuck it in his back pocket. "It could be any number of things, including a random crime. Maybe we'll find some usable prints in the house, or the stolen merchandise will turn up. I'll need you to make a list of everything that's missing."

"I don't care about that stuff. It's Patti I'm worried about."

"I'll issue a Be-On-the-Lookout for her car. If you

don't hear from her in a day or two, we can start getting worried.''

Aubrey didn't like that answer. In fact, she thought Lyle was a little cavalier about the whole thing. But he probably saw burglaries and assaults day in and day out. And people were always getting worried for nothing when their loved ones went missing, then turned up unharmed. She'd heard enough cop talk over the years to know that.

In this case, however, she was entitled to worry.

Beau could find Patti and Sara in a heartbeat. Aubrey might not approve of his methods as a bounty hunter, but it was hard to argue with his results. But his services didn't come cheap, and since assistant chemistry professors didn't make a ton of money, she didn't know how she would pay him. Still, she filed the idea away for further scrutiny.

One of the evidence technicians came out onto the porch. ''We're finished downstairs, if you want to come inside where it's cool,'' he said to Aubrey.

She was grateful he'd been kind enough to think of her, but her gratitude ended abruptly when she saw the condition of her living room. Fine black fingerprint powder coated everything.

Lyle followed her inside. ''I know a cleaning service that's pretty good at straightening up after our guys trash a place. I'll write it down for you.''

''Thanks.''

The phone rang. Aubrey didn't feel like talking to anyone, but she couldn't just let it ring. She went to the kitchen and picked up the wall phone, getting black powder on her hand. ''Hello?''

''Aubrey. Oh, my God, are you okay?''

''Patti!''

Lyle looked up sharply.

"Where are you?" Aubrey demanded, relief warring with irritation. As usual, Patti had managed to create some drama. "What's going on?"

"I'm okay. I got out before—"

"Well, I didn't! Someone broke into the house and attacked me. You knew, and you just let me walk right into it!" The tears Aubrey had been holding at bay came on full force.

"Are you hurt?" Patti asked in a small voice.

"Not seriously." Aubrey swallowed, getting the tears under control. "Why did you call me home if—"

"I don't understand. He was after me, not you. Why would he hurt you?"

"Who? Damn it, Patti, who are we talking about?"

"You'll just get mad if I tell you."

"I'm already mad. He could have killed me. Is it Charlie?"

Patti hesitated. "I'll tell you all about it later, okay? I just didn't want you to worry about me. I might not come home for a couple of days. Oh, damn, my batteries are going."

"Patti, don't hang up. Tell me who! I won't get mad, I promise," Aubrey tried in a last-ditch effort to get Patti to talk. But the connection went dead.

Lyle was listening intently. "Did she say?"

"No." Aubrey hung up. "But at least I know she's safe for now, anyway. But this wasn't just a random crime. Patti said someone was after her."

"Sounds like you were just in the wrong place at the wrong time."

Aubrey swallowed down her irritation with Lyle. She waited until the cops left, then unearthed her phone book so she could look up the number for First

Strike Bounty Hunters, a gesture which turned out to be wholly unnecessary. Beau was at her front door.

She let him in. "How did you know I was trying to call you?"

His eyebrows rose as he entered her filthy living room. "*You* were calling *me?*"

"I want you to find Patti and Sara for me. You could probably do it in your sleep."

He looked around her house, his attentive gaze missing nothing, but he didn't reply right away to her request. "They sure did a number on your house. The cops, I mean."

"They were just doing their job. Now, how about if you do your job? Will you take the case or not? I think Patti's in trouble. She called, but she sounded really strange and she wouldn't tell me—"

"She called?"

"Just a few minutes ago. She said she was safe, but—"

"Aubrey, I'm sure she's fine. You know Patti. She's a drama queen. Whatever's going on with her, she's blowing it out of proportion and creating a mystery so you'll worry."

"Maybe," Aubrey said grudgingly. "But she's changed a lot since Sara came along. She's more responsible, more considerate. She even has a job at an insurance company. Couldn't you try to find her? There's an innocent baby involved."

"If she hasn't turned up by tomorrow, let me know."

Aubrey narrowed her eyes. "Oh, I get it. There's no huge bounty on Patti's head, so it's not worth your time."

"It's not that—"

"Of course it is. Big payoffs are all that motivate you anymore. And since I don't have anything to offer you—" She broke off when she saw the appraising look in Beau's eyes.

"Oh, I don't know," he said in a lazy drawl. "I think you might have something I want."

Aubrey felt the air rush out of her lungs in a swoosh as her every hair follicle wiggled with awareness. He'd never shown the slightest interest in her before. But the way he was looking at her now, practically…what was that old cliché? Undressing her with his eyes?

She felt a little thrill at the idea that he might want her, but quickly squelched it. The very idea was hideous—trading sex for his professional services.

The corner of his mouth twitched up in what passed for a smile with Beau. "Not that. Get your mind out of the gutter."

She shook herself. What was she thinking? "What, then?" The question came out a breathy whisper.

"I want you to put the past behind us. Admit that maybe you don't understand what happened between me and Gavin, and give me the benefit of the doubt."

"It's hard to misinterpret a bullet in the leg."

"It could have been through his heart. He was pointing a weapon at me first."

"So you say. Forget it, Beau. I can't forgive you for what you did to Gavin. Not now, not ever."

"Then I guess there's nothing more to talk about. I stopped to see if you were really okay, but it appears you are. So I'm out of here."

As he sauntered away, Aubrey had to bite her lip to keep from calling him back.

Chapter Two

Aubrey couldn't wait to take a shower, to get the intruder's feel and smell off of her, to wash the blood out of her hair—and to wash that insane exchange with Beau out of her system. She carefully locked her doors, checked that the windows were secure, then headed for the upstairs bathroom.

A few minutes later, feeling much better, Aubrey decided to tackle the mess the police had made. She could have called the cleaning service Lyle recommended, but the idea of letting more strangers into her house bothered her. This cozy frame house, once her grandmother's, had always been her haven, her cocoon, in which she could shut out the rest of the world and focus for hours at a time on an obscure chemical equation, or grade papers, or read nineteenth-century chemistry texts, her favorite hobby.

Now she preferred to set things right herself, restoring each object to its correct place, buffing the old mahogany coffee table to a mirrorlike shine.

When she moved into the dining room, which had been converted to her home office, she immediately spotted something odd. A fat white envelope sat in the exact middle of her desk with her name on it. It was in Patti's writing. How had she not noticed it before?

The envelope wasn't sealed, and Aubrey opened it and withdrew the contents. The moment she read the first words on the first page, her breath caught in her throat. It was Patti's last will and testament, drawn up by her father's law firm and dated only a week previous.

That in itself was weird. Patti had been estranged from her wealthy father for many years. Why had she suddenly felt she needed to go to him for a will? The implications were ominous.

Aubrey scanned the document. Patti had apparently left everything to her daughter. That made sense. But she'd also made provisions for Aubrey to be named as Sara's guardian. The gesture brought Aubrey to tears, especially given the uncharitable thoughts she'd had about Patti in the last few hours.

"Patti, girl, you better not need this," Aubrey murmured as she tucked the will into her file cabinet.

The phone rang, startling her. She fumbled with the receiver. "Hello?"

"Do you have the money yet?" The voice was rough and low, and the words sent a chill wiggling up Aubrey's spine.

"Who are you trying to reach?" Aubrey demanded, though she was pretty sure she knew. Callers often mistook her voice for Patti's.

"Patti, Patti, Patti. After all that's been between us, you're not pretending you don't know me, are you?" the caller cooed, his voice taking on a whispery, singsong quality.

"This isn't Patti," Aubrey insisted. "She's not

here. Who is this?'' She checked her caller ID. The number had been blocked.

A long silence followed. Aubrey thought at first the caller had hung up. But then his creepy voice assaulted her again. ''Whoever you are, chicky, you tell little Patti something for me. Tell her I'm coming for her. I want my money now. She knows what'll happen if I don't get it.''

The line went dead.

Aubrey hung up and immediately dialed the police again, asking for Lyle. She was soon patched through to his cell phone. He listened attentively.

''Did he make any threats?''

''Not explicitly, but dire consequences were certainly implied.''

''We can't really do anything unless this guy makes a move.''

''What? He already made a move!'' Aubrey paced back and forth in front of her desk. ''Or did you forget so quickly that I was assaulted?''

''We don't know it's the same person.''

''Of *course* it's the same person,'' Aubrey said impatiently. ''Can't you put a trace on the call? Something?''

''Sure, we can check it out. But he's probably calling from a cell phone. Meanwhile, is there anywhere else you could stay for a few days?''

Aubrey hated the idea of abandoning her home to the Fates. But she reluctantly agreed she could stay with friends for a couple of days, until Patti came home and this mess got straightened out. She could have her home phone calls forwarded to her cell, in case Patti tried to call again.

''Try not to worry too much,'' Lyle said, his voice

soothing. "These things have a way of blowing over. These bad guys, they don't want to work too hard. So if you make things the least bit challenging for them, they move on to greener pastures pretty quick."

Aubrey was only slightly reassured by Lyle's words. Sure, he'd been a cop for a few years, and he probably knew what he was talking about. But he wasn't the one who still had a headache from her last brush with this particular bad guy.

As she packed up a few things, and a load of books to keep her occupied—she wasn't teaching at all this summer—she considered which of her friends she would impose on. Or she could drive down and stay with her parents, who had retired to South Padre Island on the Texas coast. But she didn't want to put anyone else in the line of fire. And she wanted to stay close. She wouldn't rest easy until she saw Patti and cuddled Sara in her arms.

A motel was the answer. She would stay at her favorite little hole in the wall, the Golden Sands, where she'd hidden out when she wrote both her master's thesis and her doctoral dissertation. She'd had a little problem meeting deadlines back then, and her solution was to push it as far as she could, then check into the motel and write eighteen hours a day until the thing was done, ordering out Chinese food or pizza for every meal.

The motel was only a couple of blocks from campus, near a busy intersection. She requested a room facing Eighth Street, the main drag, where her door would be very visible to anyone passing by. This might even be kind of fun, she thought as she slid her credit card to the multipierced young woman at the front desk. She could turn the air-conditioning up, swim in the tacky little pool out back, watch trashy movies or noodle around with equations.

Maybe if she distracted herself enough, she wouldn't worry so much about Patti and Sara.

With her maroon duffel bag in one hand and her key in the other, Aubrey coaxed the lock and opened the door. The room was stuffy, but she'd soon remedy that. She switched on the light, turned toward the window unit, then froze.

There was a man sitting on her bed.

She inhaled to scream until it registered that the man was Beau. He lounged against the pillows as if he had a perfect right to be there.

"What—how—what—"

"You're usually a bit more articulate, Aubrey."

Instead of trying to push one of the dozen questions she had for him out of her mouth, she folded her arms and stared until the silence became uncomfortable.

"I drove past your house again and saw you throw a duffel in the back of your Jeep," he said with a shrug. "I'll admit it, I was curious. Were you spooked? Had you found out where Patti was? I was worried, so I followed you here. If you're trying to keep yourself safe, you're not doing a very good job. Any kid with a credit card could break into these rooms."

"How did you know which room I would be in?"

"I was standing right behind you at the front desk. You never even knew I was there, so I thought I would teach you a lesson."

"You've made your point," she said, dropping her duffel and sinking into the room's only chair. She should be furious at his high-handedness—except he was right.

"Anyone could have followed you. Don't you ever check your rearview mirror? I practically tailgated you the whole way over."

Jeez. How unobservant could she be?

"You were right, I got spooked," she said, defeated. Arguing with Beau would get her nowhere. "Patti got a phone call from some creep. Apparently she owes him some money." She clenched her hands in her lap to keep them from shaking. "But there's no reason anyone would be after me. I figured once I was away from the house, I'd be fine."

"So what did the caller say?" Beau prodded her.

"He said he was coming after her to get his money, and Patti would know what would happen if she disappointed him. Something like that."

"How much money does she owe this guy?" he asked.

"I don't know, but it must be more than I could come up with easily, or she would have asked me for it."

"What about her father? Or her brother? They've both got plenty of money."

"I doubt she would ask, and even if she did, I doubt either one of them would lift a finger to help. She's hardly spoken to Uncle Wayne or David for years."

"But if she believes her life is in danger…"

Aubrey looked pensive. "I should check with them, I guess. She had a will drawn up recently at Uncle Wayne's firm, though that doesn't mean she dealt with her father or brother directly."

Beau sat up, abandoning his lounging-tiger pose. "Let's get back to the phone call. Did the guy threaten you or Patti?"

"Not in so many words. That's the same thing Lyle asked."

"So you already called the cops. That was going to be my next suggestion."

"For all the good it did. Lyle's the one who advised me to get out of the house for a while until all this blows over. He said he'd try to track down the caller."

"They always say that. I'll lay you odds he never traces the call."

"What have you got against Lyle, anyway?"

"He's a lousy cop, that's all. The business that Gavin got caught in—"

"Don't talk about Gavin to me."

"Lyle was in it up to his eyeballs," Beau continued, glossing over her sudden anger. "But no one could prove it." And then the jerk had gotten a promotion. Life wasn't fair.

Aubrey got up and paced. Beau caught a whiff of her fragrance, perfume, or maybe just shampoo or lotion. Whatever it was, he liked it—way too much. He'd thought Aubrey Schuyler was long out of his system. But seeing her again had reawakened cravings that really weren't useful at the moment. In fact, they'd never been useful, except to distract him from sleep on lonely nights.

"If some guy was threatening Patti, why didn't *she* call the cops?" he asked, following Aubrey with his eyes. She moved nice. He liked the play of muscles beneath her snug denim shorts, and the way he could see her shoulder blades whenever she lifted her mass of curls off her neck.

"She doesn't want the police involved, and I don't blame her. After all her arrests and whatnot, she has no reason to feel good about cops. Anyway, social services keeps a close watch on her, and she's worried they'll take her baby away from her.''

''Maybe they should.''

''No,'' Aubrey said fiercely. ''Patti doesn't deserve that. She's grown up a lot since you last knew her. She's off drugs, working and paying her bills. She's trying really hard to be a good mother, and she loves Sara. It's just that her past is catching up with her.''

''A past is a pretty hard thing to escape,'' Beau said. Then he sighed, hating what he was about to say. ''You want me to try to track down that phone call for you?''

''Lyle said—''

''Lyle might or might not get around to it. Besides, he has to follow certain rules, protecting privacy and all that. I don't.''

''You can do that? Trace a call?''

''Not me, but Lori Bettencourt. Her father was one of the founders of First Strike.''

''Glenn Bettencourt? The one who was killed last year?''

''Yeah. Lori's father didn't want her anywhere near the agency, but now that he's gone, she's there every day, begging for scraps. Ace—he's the guy in charge now—got her started skip-tracing. She was a quick study, and pretty soon she was on the payroll. She already had a background in computers, but now she can rival any hacker out there. She'll find out who made that call.''

''Let's make it happen, then.''

''One rule, though.''

Aubrey sighed. ''I knew this was too easy.''

''If I help you out, you do what I say. No more

staying in sleazy motels with crummy locks and a clerk who could be bought for a pack of cigarettes.''

"What alternative do you suggest?"

"We'll work out something. Maybe you could stay with Lori."

Aubrey wrinkled her nose at that, but she didn't object.

"Bring your bag, you won't be coming back here. But we'll leave your car, on the off chance it'll throw someone off the scent."

Aubrey looked as though she wanted to object to the way Beau had suddenly taken control, but again, she didn't. She must be plenty scared, Beau thought grimly, to throw in her lot with him and let him call all the shots.

Once they were in his car, Beau put the top down. The sun's full heat beat down on them, but it was worth it because he got to watch out of the corner of his eye as Aubrey tried to control her windblown curls.

"If you're able to track this guy down, what will you do with him?" she asked. "Will you turn his name over to Lyle?"

"Hah! No, I'll handle him myself. Once he realizes he's not dealing with defenseless women, that you and Patti have an ex-cop on your side, he'll be a bit more patient about getting his money."

"Do you really think so?" Aubrey asked hopefully.

"Sure. The guy sounds like a bully, and bullies run and hide when anyone stronger than they are comes around."

Aubrey flashed him a grateful smile, and it just about melted his insides. When was the last time Aubrey had actually smiled at him?

Hell, he really needed to pull his mind out of the

past. Aubrey had been his first real crush, the first girl whose opinion of him had ever mattered. She'd just turned fourteen, and she was all legs and budding breasts and lips that were unconsciously pouty. He'd casually mentioned to Gavin he might like to take Aubrey out, now that he had a driver's license and an old wreck of a car. Gavin had pushed him up against a wall and threatened to kill him if he so much as looked at his sister. It was the first time Gavin had ever directed his temper toward Beau, and it had unnerved him. Not that he was afraid, exactly. He probably could have beat Gavin to a pulp. But he didn't like seeing that side of his buddy, his best friend. Rather than provoke that sleeping beast inside Gavin again, Beau had limited himself to covert looks at Aubrey— and an active fantasy life. There were plenty of other girls who wanted to ride in his car, he'd reasoned.

They rode the rest of the way in silence, and Beau forced himself to focus on Patti's predicament. He'd known Patti well when they were kids, all of them hanging out together. As Gavin Schuyler's best friend, he'd been treated practically as one of the family, and he had always been welcome at the Schuylers' house as well as at the Clarendon home—a mansion, really. Wayne Clarendon came from old money, and he didn't hesitate to flaunt it.

Once Beau left the police force, though, his relationship with Gavin, and hence the entire family, had grown tense, and he hadn't seen much of them after that. What he did remember of Patti, though, was a weak, self-indulgent young woman prone to histrionics and a master of manipulation. Aubrey had always been vulnerable to her cousin's hijinks, because Aubrey was kind and willing to give people the benefit of the doubt.

Everyone except him.

Aubrey had *said* Patti was more mature now, but Aubrey tended to see the best in everyone, even when it wasn't deserved. Why she wanted to believe the worst about him was no mystery—he'd shot her brother, after all. But he wished she'd cut him a break.

Beau wheeled the Mustang into a parking space in front of a run-down shopping center in one of the worst parts of town.

"Why are we stopping here?" Aubrey asked with some alarm.

"This is it."

Aubrey followed his gaze to a tattered blue awning that featured *First Strike* in barely discernible white letters. Next to it was the image of a coiled snake, ready to strike. The office itself was housed in perhaps twenty feet of storefront, with steel bars covering windows streaked so dirty she couldn't see a thing inside. On one side was Bloodgood's Pawn Shop. On the other was Taft Bail Bonds.

She made no move to get out of the car.

"Aubrey, what's the holdup?"

She shook herself. What had she expected, anyway? Beau Maddox wasn't Remington Steele. "Coming."

Inside it was worse than Aubrey had feared. The office was bigger than it appeared from the outside, narrow and deep. A battered reception desk sat near the door, unoccupied at the moment, but a half-full bottle of Dr Pepper sitting on it indicated the occupant wasn't far away. A couple of other desks were arranged haphazardly around the main room, all of them messy but currently unused. In one corner was a home gym—a weight bench and a couple of machines with torn, blue-sparkle vinyl upholstery. The floor was partially covered with nasty blue indoor-outdoor carpeting, except where the concrete floor showed through huge rips and holes. The walls had been flat white once upon a time. Now they were dingy with fingerprints and God-knew-what.

A huge garbage can near the exact center of the room was full to overflowing with beer bottles and pizza cartons. Several beer bottles were strewn about the rest of the place as if it were a decorating statement. The acoustic tiles on the ceiling—the ones that weren't missing—were stained and crumbling, and the ancient fluorescent light fixtures bathed the entire nightmare in anemic blue light.

One wall was entirely covered in Wanted posters. Several of the scary faces peering out from those posters had darts protruding from them.

"This place is completely gross," Aubrey couldn't help saying. "How can you stand working here?"

Beau smiled and shrugged as he looked around. "I don't spend much time here, really. Hey," he called out, "is anyone here?"

A door in the back opened and a striking woman close to Aubrey's age appeared. She was tall, slender and large-breasted, but ultracasual in a snug black tank top, low-slung camouflage cargo pants and flip-flops. Her honey-blond hair was cut in a short, no-nonsense style, and she wore little if any makeup, which in no way detracted from her very feminine appearance.

She smiled at Beau. "Sorry, I was just in the bathroom," she said without embarrassment. "Ace isn't here, if that's who you're looking for. Who's this?" She turned her winning smile on Aubrey.

Aubrey liked this woman immediately. She held out her hand. "Aubrey Schuyler."

"Lori Bettencourt," the other woman said, gripping Aubrey's hand firmly. "I know this place is disgusting, and I apologize. But I told Ace when I came to work here that being a maid wasn't part of my job description just because I'm the only woman. I clean up after myself and I try not to look at the rest. Though I do carry around a big bottle of Lysol."

Aubrey found herself smiling back. "I like your attitude."

"Actually," Beau said, "I'm not looking for Ace. I'm looking for you."

"Really? Need some help with a takedown?" she asked hopefully.

Aubrey watched Lori closely, trying to figure out if there was anything sexual between her and Beau. Not that it should matter. She didn't give a rat's behind who Beau slept with, she told herself sternly. But she found she was relieved when her radar didn't pick up any sexual undercurrents between the two, though they obviously liked one another.

"Aubrey got a threatening phone call. I want you to trace it."

Lori looked disappointed. "Just a phone call? Piece of cake." She led the way to the desk farthest back from the front door, on which sat what looked to be an ancient computer with half its guts hanging out. But once Lori fired up the machine, Aubrey could see it was endowed with a powerful CPU and lots of state-of-the-art software.

Aubrey gave Lori her phone number and the approximate time of the call, then left her alone to do her thing.

"Is it legal, what she's doing?" she asked Beau, who'd decided to pass the time by doing a few chin-ups on a bar that was part of the home gym.

"Beats me. I don't care, long as she doesn't get caught."

That was typical, she thought, frowning. Beau seemed to have lost any semblance of a conscience once he'd left the police force. She reminded herself of that as she forced herself to stop watching his bulging biceps as he lifted his weight up and down in a seemingly tireless set.

The door from which Lori had emerged opened again, and a robust-looking man in his fifties appeared. "Hey, Lori, you want to do a—" He stopped when he spotted Beau. "Maddox. You find that Langford kid yet?"

"I've been checking out the day-care centers," Beau replied, sounding unconcerned. "Nothing yet."

The older man's eyes locked on Aubrey. "Who's this?"

"Aubrey Schuyler. Lori's tracing a call for her. Aubrey, this is Ace McCullough. He owns the agency."

Ace McCullough grinned, revealing two even rows of very white teeth. "Schuyler, Schuyler. Why does that name sound familiar?"

"Gavin Schuyler's my brother."

That seemed to be enough explanation. Ace quickly changed the subject. "Lori, will you be done pretty quick? I have an easy takedown, and I thought you might want to come with me."

Lori's eyes lit up with something Aubrey could only describe as yearning. "This won't take long," she assured Ace. "Don't go without me."

Beau finally tired of his chin-ups. Though he was

hardly breathing hard, he did have a sheen of perspiration on his forehead. He picked up a towel that someone had slung over a barbell and wiped his face and neck with it. Aubrey shuddered to think about where that towel had been, or how long it had gone without seeing the inside of a washing machine.

"Are you sure you're doing the right thing?" Beau asked Ace in a soft voice. "With Lori, I mean. Glenn really didn't want her here. Anyway, she's just a kid."

"She's twenty-seven, hardly a kid," Ace countered. "I don't want to dishonor Glenn's memory by going against his wishes, but Lori's got bounty-hunting in her blood. If I hadn't taken her in, she would have gone to work for some other agency—or worse, she'd have tried working on her own. At least if she's working here, I can train her right, and keep an eye on her. And you have to admit, her computer skills have come in handy."

"I guess you're right," Beau said grudgingly.

"Right now, I'm only letting her do the easy takedowns. This one's an old lady with parking tickets who missed her court date, probably because she's senile."

Beau smiled. "Doesn't sound too bad, though I once had a senile little old lady pull a Luger on me."

The two men laughed, but Aubrey didn't join in. The thought of the kind of danger Beau put himself in every day was intimidating. At least as a cop, he had the full weight of the law behind him and plenty of backup just a radio summons away. By his own account, when he'd been on the force he'd never even fired his weapon, or been fired at.

As a bounty hunter, his job was far riskier. Every day he went looking for trouble. She just didn't understand why anyone would submit himself to that much risk. The Beau Maddox she'd known wasn't an adrenaline junkie.

Aubrey returned her attention to Lori, who was scribbling something down on a piece of paper. Lori looked up.

"Bad news. The call came from a pay phone."

Chapter Three

Beau cursed softly, and Aubrey sagged with her own disappointment. Finding the guy who'd assaulted her and threatened Patti wasn't going to be easy. But she realized she would never feel completely safe until the guy was behind bars, and Patti and Sara were home where they belonged.

"I wrote the pay phone address down," Lori said. "It's not far from here, if you want to check it out." She walked over and handed the piece of paper to Beau with the location of the pay phone. Then she looked at Ace. "Just let me get my stuff, and I'll be ready."

Aubrey was about to say thanks and slide on out of there herself. But her car was still at the motel.

"It's only a few blocks," Beau said. "We can walk over and have a look. Chances are our guy lives or works close by. The information might help us narrow the search if we get any more leads on this scumbag."

When Lori returned from her desk up front, she wore a bulletproof vest. She had a Mace canister in one of the loops of her cargo pants, and an impossibly huge gun secured at the small of her back.

"Put a shirt on over that vest," Beau said, looking

as if he had to struggle to keep from laughing. "You might as well be wearing a neon sign over your head, Bounty Hunter In Training."

Lori shot him a dirty look, but she did as he suggested.

Once they were back outside, Aubrey was relieved to be breathing fresh air again. "I don't know how she stands it," she said to Beau as they set out to find the pay phone.

"Lori? How she stands what?"

"That place you work at. It's repulsive. Might as well be working in a men's locker room. I'm surprised there wasn't dirty laundry all over the floor."

Beau only grinned. "You didn't see the back room. Or the kitchen. It's enough to make a health inspector faint."

"You sound almost proud."

"Hey, it took us years to get that place to such a high degree of disreputableness."

Aubrey gave up. Men were disgusting. She should probably be glad she hadn't yet married one. Maybe she never would.

The block where the pay phone was located was even worse than the one that housed First Strike. Aubrey spotted several seedy-looking bars, a head shop, an adult bookstore, an adult video store, an out-of-business dry cleaner, a thrift store and a dollar store. Judging from the clientele she saw loitering in various doorways, this was the neighborhood where the more adventurous college students from University of East Texas hung out. If she recognized any of *her* students here, she was going to call their mothers.

"Hey, my man, what's happening?" A young African-American man came out of a doorway to give Beau a high five.

"Hey, Junior."

"You know these people?" Aubrey whispered after they'd passed.

"Some of them. Finding fugitives requires information, sometimes from the less-elevated echelons of society. So I make it a point to get to know these folks. They'll tell me stuff they'd never tell a cop."

The pay phone was in use, and it appeared to have a line of young men waiting to use it.

"Is there something special about this phone?" she asked.

"Kids use it for dealing drugs and calling prostitutes," Beau explained. "They don't want any numbers they can't explain showing up on the cell phone bill Mom and Dad pay every month."

"You'd think the police would do something!" Aubrey said, indignant.

"It's not against the law to use the phone."

"They could follow these kids. Find out who they're buying drugs from. Or selling drugs to."

"Too labor-intensive. Not enough manpower. Not enough budget. They'd rather spend their time arresting speeders and kids making U-turns at the wrong time of day. Easy arrests that pump up the statistics and fill the coffers."

Aubrey realized she'd hit a nerve with Beau.

"Besides, if the cops tried to clean up this area, all my good snitches would be gone." He seemed to enjoy the look of distaste on Aubrey's face. But then he grew serious. "Look around. See anyone familiar hanging around the pay phone?"

Aubrey covertly studied the faces of the kids. "No."

"How about any of the businesses around here? Ever remember Patti mentioning any of them?"

Aubrey studied each seedy little bar and bookstore. Finally she saw something that jogged her memory. "That bar over there, the one called Kink?"

"Yeah?"

"I think Patti used to be a waitress there, but it was a while ago."

"Still, that might be the link we're looking for."

"Let's go check it out." She turned, but Beau grabbed her arm before she could get going.

"Wait. You know what kind of bar that is?"

"What do you mean? One that serves alcohol, I presume."

"It's an S&M bar."

That stopped her cold. "You mean, like sadism and masochism?"

"I mean, people who dress in leather and studs and stick safety pins in parts of their bodies you don't even want to think about. Outsiders aren't welcome, and no one would tell us a thing. I might pass, but you'd stick out like a nun in a cathouse."

"I beg your pardon. I can pass for sleazy and deviant if I want to."

Beau just shook his head. "Not you, Squeak."

"You know I *hate* that nickname." Squeak stood for Squeaky Clean. Beau and Gavin had come up with it when she was in junior high, and they'd used it whenever they thought she was being too goody-goody.

"They're not even open this time of day. We can go back later tonight, if you want. But we'll have to dress the parts. Lori can probably help us out. She's got all kinds of disguises.''

"Really."

"She's good at undercover work." Beau took Aubrey's arm and led her down the sidewalk. "We've been standing in one place too long. Don't want to attract attention." They headed away from the pay phone.

"Beau, does this mean I've hired you?"

"What?"

"Well, you were just doing me a favor to trace the number, and I appreciate it. But beyond that…" She shrugged. "I know you guys charge a fortune for your services. And I don't have a fortune."

His face clouded. "You don't owe me a damn thing. I happen to have some time to kill, that's all."

"What about that Langford kid Ace mentioned? Shouldn't you be looking for him?"

"I've *been* looking for him." Frustration rose in Beau's voice. "I have a lead, but I can't do anything about it until tomorrow morning. Hey, I don't tell you how to teach chemistry, okay?"

"Fine." She determinedly walked ten paces ahead of him. Though she was tempted to call a cab and return to her motel, wash her hands completely of Beau Maddox, she knew she'd be a fool to turn down his help while he was willing to give it. If he made her uncomfortable, it was a small price to pay for getting his services for free.

As she turned the corner, she noticed a couple of young women sitting on a car, drinking sodas and talking in loud voices. They wore extremely short skirts, tight tank tops with no bras, excessive costume jewelry, big hair and tons of makeup. As soon as Aubrey realized what she was looking at, she averted her gaze and quickened her step.

Jeez, right here in broad daylight!

"Hey, Beau!" one of the women called out. Aubrey froze and turned around. Sure enough, Beau had stopped to talk with the women. Should she walk on? Should she stand a discreet distance away and wait for him to finish his chat?

Finally she decided she was being silly and judgmental. They might be prostitutes, but she still owed them simple courtesy. She approached the car, and Beau angled his body out to include her in the group.

"Jodie, Erin, this is my friend, Aub—"

"Dr. Schuyler!" the one called Erin exclaimed. "Oh, my God. I had you for freshman chemistry!"

The other girl, Jodie, smirked. "You took chemistry?"

"Well, I flunked." Erin turned back to Aubrey. "Remember me?"

"Two years ago," Aubrey said as the memory came to her. "You sat in the back row and slept."

Erin smiled broadly. "You do remember. What are you doing hanging out with this guy?" She nudged Beau with her foot.

Beau slid his arm around Aubrey. "What, I'm not allowed to have a respectable girlfriend?"

"Nuh-uh," Jodie said. "I'm your girlfriend, forever and ever. You promised."

"I'm not his girlfriend," Aubrey objected, but in the face of all that overt sex appeal being directed at Beau, she almost wished she could put a claim on him. The feel of his arm around her waist was warm and secure, causing an unwelcome shiver to wiggle up her spine in spite of the afternoon heat.

"Hey, we're just kidding around," Erin said, apparently sensing Aubrey's unease. But Beau kept his arm where it was. Maybe it was a gesture of protection, a sign to these girls that they weren't supposed to mess with her.

"Hey, Beau, did I hear you were looking for Shelley?" Jodie asked.

Beau shrugged. "Yeah, I was," he said with seeming disinterest. But the tension suddenly radiating out of his arm and hand was palpable.

"What's it worth to you?"

"The usual."

"How about double the usual?"

"How about I tell your brother you're turning tricks on Chestnut Street?"

"Beau! Okay. Twenty now, and fifty if my tip is good."

"Sounds reasonable." He shook her hand, and Jodie adjusted the strap of her tank top. Aubrey realized the transaction had already taken place.

"She's staying at her aunt's house, in that new subdivision on Monument Hill. It's a redbrick house with a broken mailbox."

"Thanks. I'll let you know if it pans out."

"I know you will."

Beau started to lead Aubrey away, but she hesitated. She looked at Erin, who couldn't meet her gaze.

"Don't say it, Dr. Schuyler," she mumbled. "It's nothing I haven't heard before."

When they were a block away, Aubrey finally spoke. "That is so sad. We should be doing something to help them, instead of paying them for tips."

"Erin's been dragged off to rehab twice. We can't force her to change."

"Like Patti, I guess," Aubrey said on a sigh. "She didn't want to change until Sara came along."

They stopped at a corner for a light, and Aubrey felt light-headed all the sudden. She reached out for a lamppost to steady herself.

Beau looked at her with concern. "When was the last time you ate?"

She had to think about it. She'd eaten a bagel for breakfast, a lifetime ago, and she'd thrown up since then. No wonder she was cranky. "I'm not sure I could eat anything."

"Sure you can." He steered her into a pancake house a couple of blocks from the agency. "You can't do this kind of work without fuel for your brain, not to mention your body." He nodded to the hostess, then guided Aubrey to a booth in the back. A wispy-haired waitress appeared.

"Your usual, Beau?" She cocked her hip to one side and blushed furiously.

"Yeah. You want a menu, Aubrey?"

"No. Just some wheat toast and hot tea."

The waitress disappeared, then returned with coffee for Beau and Aubrey's tea.

"I'm gonna run down to the agency and check on a few things," Beau said. "I'll be back before the food gets here. Meanwhile, I want you to get on your cell phone and call everyone you can think of who knows Patti—friends, relatives, co-workers, neighbors, former lovers, anybody. See if you can get a lead on where she might be hiding out, or who she owed money to." He slid out of the booth and disappeared, seemingly confident Aubrey would obey orders.

With a sigh she got out her cell phone and a small address book she kept in her purse. She knew hardly any of Patti's friends. Though they'd lived together for more than a year—since Charlie Soffit had kicked Patti out of his mobile home—Aubrey knew very little of Patti's life. But she had Charlie's phone number. That was a start. And the number at the insurance agency where Patti worked.

First, though, she wanted to call her uncle Wayne. Since Patti had gone to his law firm for the will, he might know something. Besides, she hadn't talked to that branch of the family in months. Since her parents had retired to Padre, her uncle and cousin David were the only family she had left in town, other than Patti and Sara. Yet she hardly ever talked to them. She'd once been pretty close to David, who was her own age. Back when they were kids, she and David had been the "good kids," the scaredy-cats who'd tried to keep the others—Gavin, Beau and Patti—from getting into trouble. Now, though, they didn't have much in common. He'd gone to William and Mary, then law school. They moved in different circles.

She dialed Uncle Wayne's home number. This time of the afternoon, he would probably be there. He was semiretired from the firm now, only rarely visiting the office.

She was surprised when David answered the phone.

"Aubrey. How in the hell are you?"

"I'm…okay," she said guardedly, not wanting to blurt out that she'd been assaulted, her home had been burglarized, and that his sister and niece were missing. "Shouldn't you be at work?"

"God knows I should be. But…" His voice trailed off. He sounded troubled.

"What is it, David?"

"I probably should have called you. Dad's not doing too well. He has cancer."

"Oh, my God, that's awful! Is he…I mean, lots of people survive…."

"Not this time. It's all over his body. They're not even sure where it started. They caught it way too late to do anything. He's got a couple of months at most."

Aubrey took a sip of her tea, trying to absorb the terrible news. "You should have let me know."

"He didn't want me to. He didn't want everyone to worry about him. You know how he is."

"It's my fault, too. I should have kept in better touch. I mean, a card and a canister of cookies at Christmas…"

"Well, it's been awkward, with Patti living with you."

This was true. Patti had a way of putting tension on the whole family, making Aubrey feel like a traitor if she got too friendly with the enemy.

"Could I talk to Uncle Wayne?"

"Um, not right now. He's sedated. That's why I'm not at work. He's having a really bad day. When he's like this, I don't feel right just leaving him with the nurse and the housekeeper. In fact, I've moved back here to care for him."

"I'm so sorry." It was all she could think of to say. David and Patti had lost their mother to lung cancer when they were just teenagers. Aubrey had always believed it was losing her mother so young that had caused Patti to rebel. "I wanted to ask Uncle Wayne something, but you might be able to help me. Patti's gotten herself in a bit of trouble."

"This is news?" She could almost see him rolling his eyes.

"Seriously, David. She had a will drawn up at the firm just in the past few weeks. I thought maybe she might have told you or Uncle Wayne what the problem was."

"She owes somebody some money."

"Then you know? You've talked to her?"

"I didn't know anything about the will. But I did talk to her. She called here a couple of days ago, wanting to speak to Dad. I didn't let her—his doctor says he shouldn't get upset, and Patti can't talk to Dad without upsetting him. Then she told me she needed some money."

"You didn't give it to her, I take it."

"Of course not. She's always making up sob stories about how she needs money. This time she said she'd borrowed money from a loan shark, and he was going to put a contract on her life if she didn't pay him off. It's not...I mean, it's not true, is it?" His voice showed sudden concern.

"I think it might be. Certainly there's a very unpleasant person looking for her. And she's missing. She took Sara and fled."

"Aw, hell. Aubrey, I didn't know, I swear it. She's cried wolf so many times—"

"I know, David. I don't blame you." She told him then about the break-in and the assault, and the spooky phone call.

"Jeez, Aubrey. Are you safe now? You can stay with us if you want. We have burglar bars and a good security system. We had a prowler a while back, a real creepy guy peeking in the windows, and Dad got paranoid. This house is like Fort Knox now."

"I might take you up on that. So you haven't seen Patti since you talked to her a couple of days ago?"

"No. I haven't seen her in months."

"She might just show up there and try to see her dad. If she does, call me right away, okay?"

"Of course. Hell, I'll help her if I can. I just had no idea."

"I know. Give my love to your dad, will you? And tell him I'll visit soon."

Aubrey hung up and took another sip of tea. Beau returned just as the food arrived. He had his timing down.

"You okay?" he asked. "You look kind of pale."

As he wolfed down pancakes, she told him about her phone call with David. Beau was visibly shaken. The Clarendons had been like family to him, once upon a time. "I haven't been the greatest about keeping in touch, either. You're not the only one who's got a bit of a grudge against me."

A grudge. That was an understatement.

"Your aunt and uncle were always really nice to me," he continued, "though I suspect they thought I was a bad influence on David."

"David? No way. He was incorruptible. 'Squeak' fits him better than me."

Beau shook his head, the corner of his mouth turning up in that infuriating almost-smile. "He had you snowed, Aubrey." But then he turned serious. "I need to check out the tip Erin gave me. You want to help me out?"

"Me?"

"It's a conservative neighborhood. I'll be spotted immediately, but you'll look right at home."

"What exactly do you want me to do?"

Beau handed the waitress money for the bill, including a generous tip, and they left the restaurant.

"Once we find the house, just go up to the door and pretend you're a new neighbor. Ask for a cup of sugar or something."

"I'll ask to use the phone."

Beau grinned. "You're a natural."

They climbed back into his Mustang. Beau raised the top and turned on the air-conditioning, for which Aubrey was extremely grateful. She normally didn't mind the Texas heat, but her fair skin would freckle if she got any more sun.

They found the small tract house with the broken mailbox soon enough. Beau parked around the corner. "If someone answers the door, try to peek inside and look for a two-year-old." He showed Aubrey a photo of a cute towheaded toddler. "If you see the kid or kid's toys, that's all I need for now."

Aubrey couldn't believe she was doing this, but it sounded easy enough. Anyway, she needed the practice. She was going undercover tonight—at an S&M bar.

A woman in her fifties answered the door. "Yes?"

"Hi, I'm Rita McMurray." She had no idea where that name had come from. "I'm moving in a couple of houses down," she said, pointing vaguely down the block, "and they haven't connected the phone yet. Could I use yours?"

The woman gave a tight smile. "Sure. I'll bring you the cordless." She closed the screen door, but Aubrey got a clear view inside. She looked for any sign of a child and saw nothing. But moments later an ear-piercing shriek rent the air. The child—for surely that's what it was—was quickly shushed by someone inside.

The woman returned with the phone. Aubrey dialed

her office number, pretended to talk to her nonexistent husband, returned the phone and got out of there. She felt triumphant, exultant, as she rounded the corner and got into Beau's car.

"Yup, there's a child in there. I didn't see him, but I heard him. And he was shushed up really quickly."

"Good work." He pulled a cell phone from the console and dialed, then gave some terse directions. Apparently he was going to extract the child from the house right now.

In fifteen minutes two more cars showed up. One held Ace and Lori. A man Aubrey had never met climbed out of the second. He was huge, six-three at least, with blond hair cut very short and piercing green eyes. He screamed ex-military.

The three men and Lori conferred on the sidewalk while Aubrey remained in the stifling car. Then the blond man and Ace went up the alley, while Beau walked back down the block toward the front of the redbrick house.

Lori joined Aubrey at the car, leaning in the open window. "Don't you just hate being a woman sometimes? Those macho jerks won't let me help."

The last place Aubrey wanted to be was with the guys right now. "I'll stay right here where it's safe, thanks."

"Come on, let's watch."

Aubrey got out of the car, though Beau had told her not to, and she and Lori peeked out from behind a fence. Beau beat on the front door. "Fugitive recovery agent! Open up!"

The door opened immediately and Beau went inside. An interminable amount of time seemed to pass, though realistically it was probably only a minute or two. Then he emerged holding a screaming child. He gave a signal to Lori.

"Come on, that's our cue."

Without knowing what she was doing, Aubrey jumped in the Mustang along with Lori, who cranked it up, put it in gear, and skidded around the corner. Beau met the car, opened Aubrey's door and handed the kid to her. "Get out of here."

Lori hit the gas.

The child screamed despite Aubrey's attempts to comfort him. "Is this legal?" she asked Lori. "Just snatching a kid away from his mother?"

"She kidnapped him first."

"But...she's his mother."

"She's a prostitute, and a junkie. We didn't take her kid away, the courts did. We're just enforcing what the court ordered."

Aubrey wasn't sure she liked it. That woman could have been Patti. Beau's career choice seemed morally ambiguous at best. But then, that was her whole objection to how Beau earned a living. He followed the cash—even if that meant betraying his best friend.

Chapter Four

Beau wasn't sure he'd done the right thing by taking Aubrey with him to extract Christopher Langford from the house. But he'd needed to act quickly. If he'd waited even a few hours, Shelley might have gotten spooked and skipped out with the kid. And he couldn't think of any place to leave Aubrey where he knew she'd be safe.

He wasn't sure when he'd decided that protecting her was his job. All he knew was that if something happened to her, he would feel directly responsible.

She might not know it, but he was on the job, whether or not she wanted to pay him. After what he'd done to Gavin, he figured he owed her and her family. The Schuylers and Clarendons had been the prevailing influence on his youth. Lord knew his own family hadn't done much for him. His mother had died when he was three and his father had spent the next fifteen years drinking himself into a premature grave.

Lori offered to take over little Christopher, return him to his father and collect the reward on Beau's behalf, and he was happy to let her. Ace was paying her a small salary to handle bureaucratic details, something all of the First Strike agents appreciated. But

once Lori was earning enough of her own fees to make
a living, they'd all have to do their own grunt work.

"That was...intense," Aubrey commented once
they were alone again. It was getting close to five
o'clock, and they sat in his car at a Sonic Drive-In.
"I can't believe we're just sitting here, drinking root
beer. You seem so casual about it."

"It's my job. And that was an easy extraction. Shelley and her aunt took one look at me and crumbled.
No guns, no chasing."

"Will Shelley get in trouble?"

Beau shrugged. "Not my problem. If my client
wants to press charges, that's his business. Hey, it's
almost five o'clock," he said, changing the subject.
"Did you say Patti had a job?"

"She works for an insurance agent, answering the
phone." Aubrey was glad to refocus her energies on
her own problems.

"Why don't we pay this agent a visit? We can probably catch him before he goes home for the day. He
might be able to tell us if Patti's had any strange visitors at work, or phone calls. She might have even
confided the problem to him, asked him to advance
her salary or something."

"It's worth a shot, though I doubt she would confide anything in him. She thinks he's a jerk."

They arrived at the Greg Holmes Insurance Agency
at five minutes to five. It was a small, one-agent operation, affiliated with one of the less prestigious national firms. The office was a bit run-down, but Beau
couldn't exactly criticize the man for his decorating
taste, given where he worked.

A plump young woman with a discreet tattoo on her
wrist looked as if she were about to leave. She stood

behind her desk, putting a yellow camp shirt on over her sleeveless blouse. Her skirt was a bit too short for office wear. In fact, with her brassy bleach job and eye makeup à la Tammy Faye, she could have hung out with Jodie and Erin and looked right at home.

"Can I help you?" she asked, not particularly friendly.

"I'm a friend of Patti Clarendon," Beau said.

"She's not here. She lit out of here this morning, no explanation, stuck me with answering the phone when I could be out making calls. Hey, are you cops or something?"

"I'm Patti's cousin," Aubrey said. "We're roommates. I'm a little bit worried about her."

Beau silently applauded her. She seemed to know just the right tone to strike with this slightly hostile young woman.

"You're Summer, right?" Aubrey continued. "Patti talks about you all the time. She says you're really good at handling people when they come in all upset."

That earned a slight smile from Summer. "People get real wacko sometimes. Usually it's because they're embarrassed they've wrecked their car."

Beau found a chair and picked up a magazine. Aubrey was handling Summer just fine. He'd let her keep going.

"When Patti left this morning, she didn't give you any indication of what was wrong?"

"She got a phone call. She's not supposed to take personal calls, but she's got that phone glued to her ear all day. Anyway, after this call, she said she had to go and she'd be gone the rest of the day. Oh, wait, I remember now. She said something about her kid being sick or something, and she had to pick her up from the baby-sitter.''

"I thought you said she didn't give an explanation," Beau couldn't help asking.

"I forgot, okay? I got better things to do than keep track of Patti's soap-opera life."

"Why do you think her life's a soap opera?" Aubrey asked.

"What, are you kidding? You live with her. She's got that gross-out ex-husband, Charlie—I think he's a serial killer in training—and she works in a topless bar and she bangs her boss." Summer covered her mouth. "Oops, I'm not supposed to know that. But if that isn't a soap opera, what is?"

Beau tensed as Aubrey's eyes got bigger with every word Summer spoke. *Come on, babe, don't blow it now.* Summer was spilling her guts to a perfect stranger. Aubrey really did have a knack for this. But she was going to blow it if she freaked out now.

To her credit, Aubrey managed a smile. "I guess my cousin is a bit colorful. But she's not as tough as she pretends. She's in trouble, but I don't want to call the cops if I don't have to."

At the mention of cops, Summer's expression closed up. "Hey, I don't know anything. But you might ask Greg. He knows Patti better than I do. Way better, if you catch my meaning."

The girl was as subtle as an army boot.

"I gotta go. Greg's in his office," she said, nodding to a closed door. "He's got a client with him, and he doesn't like to be interrupted. But he has to come out eventually."

Without any further ado, Summer pulled her purse out of a drawer and left.

Aubrey sank into the only other chair in the waiting room. "She was sleeping with her boss?" she said in a low voice, sounding appalled.

"I take it you didn't know that."

"Surely Patti would have told me if she had a new boyfriend. Anyway, she thinks Greg is a jerk. And what was that garbage about a topless bar?"

"Some of the waitresses at Kink go topless. Or almost."

"But she doesn't work there anymore."

"Does she spend all her evenings at home?"

Aubrey said nothing for a few moments. "I wonder what else she hasn't told me."

Beau stood up and moved behind the desk Summer had just abandoned. "I'm gonna see if Patti left anything helpful in her desk. This is where she usually works, right?"

"Beau!" Aubrey sounded panicky. "You can't just search her desk. What if Greg Holmes comes out here and catches you?"

Beau already had the desk drawer open. "He'll yell. Big deal."

The desk drawer held the usual office supplies— pens and pencils, stamps, rubber bands, paper clips. There were a couple of snapshots of a baby, which Beau assumed was Sara. He tucked these in his pocket. Might be useful later.

The file drawer held an array of untidy hanging folders. None of the labels sounded promising. They seemed to contain client policies. A drawer on the other side of the desk held more personal items. Beau examined and set aside a box of tissue, a bottle of antacid tablets, a couple of alternative rock CDs—and a brown envelope. He pulled out the paper inside.

"What is it?" Aubrey asked nervously.

"Looks like a copy of the document Patti's boyfriend signed, giving up his parental rights. Was she having trouble with him?"

"Not recently. Besides, that voice on the phone didn't sound like Charlie, although…I guess he could have been disguising it. The voice was kind of hoarse and whispery."

The murmured voices inside the office got louder, and the doorknob rattled. Beau quickly closed the drawer and scooted out from behind the desk. He pretended to study a picture on the wall of a clown when Greg Holmes's office door opened.

"I'll call you tomorrow and let you know," said the older of the two men who emerged from the inner office. He wore a suit—cheap and ill-fitting—and sported a determined five-o'clock shadow. His thinning hair was styled in a comb-over.

He vigorously pumped the hand of the other man, who was younger and kind of punk-looking, with ratty clothes and a scraggly beard.

The older man, whom Beau assumed was Greg Holmes, stopped suddenly. "Who are you?" he asked in a startled voice, his beady eyes focusing on Beau.

"Summer told us we could wait here," Beau said affably.

The punk looked a little nervous. He made for the exit, as if he didn't want to prolong any conversation with strangers.

"Summer knows better than to let customers sit in here unattended," he muttered angrily. Beau thought he was rather inhospitable for an insurance agent. For all Holmes knew, they could be in the market for millions of dollars' worth of life insurance.

"I'm Patti's cousin, Aubrey Schuyler," Aubrey said with a smile, extending her hand. "She's told me so much about you, Mr. Holmes."

Holmes softened a bit. Who could blame him? When Aubrey turned those liquid green eyes on a man, he couldn't help but fall in line with her wishes. He gave Aubrey's extended hand a grudging squeeze. "Is something wrong?" he asked. "She's been gone all day. I was starting to get worried about her."

"We don't know where she is," Beau said, extending his hand. He introduced himself as a friend of the family. "We were hoping you might shed some light on the situation."

"Why would I know anything?" Holmes asked, suddenly defensive. "She's just an employee. I don't know anything about her personal life."

Beau thought the man's reaction was just a bit too emphatic. "People who work together all day long often know more about each other than their own families," Beau said.

"Look, she answers my phones and does a little typing. I don't spend significant time with her. I'm much too busy with clients to socialize with the receptionist."

Beau thought Greg Holmes had just taken a giant step back from *I was starting to get worried about her.* Maybe he wanted to hide the fact he'd been sleeping with her. He wore a wedding ring.

"She apparently got a phone call this morning that alarmed her," Aubrey said gently. "We wondered if you knew who—"

"Why would I know who?" Holmes said, even more agitated. "I don't listen in on my receptionist's phone calls."

"Do you have a caller ID?" Beau asked.

"No. What right do you have—"

Beau held up his hands to slow Holmes's rampage of words. "Easy, easy. We don't have any right at all. We're just asking, and of course you can refuse us. But the sooner we locate Patti, the less likely the cops will come here looking for the same thing we are. Only, they'll have a warrant."

Aubrey gripped his arm. She obviously didn't like the sudden escalation of hostility.

Holmes backed down slightly. "I don't have any way of knowing who called."

Aubrey handed Holmes a card. "That has my cell number on it. Will you let me know if you think of anything, or if anyone else calls or comes by looking for Patti?"

Holmes took the card and stuck it in his jacket pocket. "Now, if you don't mind, I need to get home. My wife isn't feeling well." He ushered them out, then watched until they got into their car and left.

"I wouldn't be feeling well either if I was married to him," Aubrey said. "Don't you think he acted kind of suspiciously?"

"Kind of?"

"Well, he probably wasn't the one that called her. From his own office?"

"He could have buzzed her on the intercom. Summer might not have noticed the difference, if she wasn't paying attention. Could he be the one who called you?"

Aubrey thought for a moment. "I honestly don't know. But I can't imagine Patti being scared of Mr. Comb-Over. Or sleeping with him, for that matter. If he was rich, maybe…"

"Appearances can be deceiving. He might have offshore accounts bulging with undeclared income. That guy who was in his office? I think I busted him once for narcotics possession."

"Can Lori try to track down the phone call Patti received this morning?"

"Sure. But if a lot of calls come in, it might be hard to pinpoint which one it was."

Aubrey pulled out her cell phone and checked the call history. "Patti's call to me came in at 9:59 this morning. We can ask Lori to check for a call immediately preceding that."

"Okay." Beau put the Mustang's top back down. It was still hot, and the sun was a long way from setting, but at least it wasn't directly overhead anymore. "You were good in there."

"What?"

"You have a real talent for disarming people, putting them at ease and getting information out of them. If you ever want to make some extra money—"

"Oh, I don't think so." She shook her head vehemently.

"You really think what I do is so bad?"

"I think it's vile. Running around like Rambo, breaking into houses, threatening senile little old ladies with Mace—"

"That was Lori, not me."

"You work outside the legal limits and you don't answer to anyone or anything except the almighty dollar."

"Am I making any money off you?" he countered. Her criticism rankled. No, more than that. It hurt. He could tell himself a million times over that Aubrey

Schuyler's opinion of him didn't matter one iota. But it did.

Damn it, it did.

She didn't argue further. He considered pressing his point, then decided he'd quit while he was ahead. Let her think about why, exactly, he was spending his time trying to catch the guy who'd hurt her.

AUBREY DIDN'T KNOW what to think. Ever since the day Beau had shot her brother, she'd thought of him as the bad guy, the betrayer, a cynical, self-centered, macho jerk. She'd invested a lot of time and energy refining that image of him, savoring her loathing of him. Her brother could have died! As it was, he was in Huntsville serving a ten-year sentence.

Now Beau was forcing her to rethink the picture she had of him, to tamp down that passionate, self-righteous disgust she felt for his profession.

Why *was* he helping her when she'd clearly promised no monetary reward? Out of guilt? That would imply he had a conscience. The Beau Maddox she'd grown up with had definitely harbored a conscience. Sure, he'd gotten himself and Gavin involved in some youthful hijinks. A little mailbox-bashing, some graffiti on school property, underage drinking. But nothing really hurtful. In fact, once when he'd realized one of the mailboxes he'd hit with a brick belonged to a nice old widow who took in stray dogs, he'd gone to her house, admitted what he'd done and fixed her mailbox for her.

His act of thoughtfulness, albeit a little late, had been one of many things that had convinced her Beau Maddox was worthy of her undying love. Not that she'd ever confided her feelings in anyone. Gavin had warned her not to humiliate him by flirting with any of his friends. So she'd suffered in silence, not so much because she was afraid of Gavin, but because she was afraid of Beau's rejection.

At any rate, once upon a time he'd had at least a sliver of conscience. Could life have knocked that out of him completely? As a cop, he'd had a reputation for sound judgment. Gavin had privately thought Beau was a little bit soft, especially when it came to juveniles. Sometimes, instead of arresting a kid when that would be the easiest course to take, he'd dragged the kid home to a parent and spent two hours putting the fear of God into both of them.

Aubrey had admired him for that, too.

What, then, had made him turn away from the respectable job of police officer and morph into a lawless bounty hunter? Was it possible she didn't have all the pieces of the puzzle?

Thinking about it made her head hurt, and she realized she was hungry. Not just light-headed from lack of food, like earlier, but truly ravenous.

"Do you want to get a cheeseburger at Stubby's?" she asked. "My treat." It was the closest she was going to get to an apology for giving him a hard time. She wasn't ready to admit she was wrong about him, not by a long shot. But she was ready for a truce, at least long enough that she could digest some empty calories in peace.

Beau didn't answer, but he turned the car toward Stubby's, a greasy burger joint that had been around since before anyone could remember. Generations of high school kids had hung out there—bobby soxers and beatniks, hippies and urban cowboys, flash dancers, punk rockers and the latest kids that hadn't yet found their niche in history. Stubby's onion rings, in particular, were beyond compare, and whenever Aubrey ate here, it took her back to her giddy teen years.

She and Beau slid into a booth, one they'd sat in countless times before with Gavin, David, and sometimes Patti when she was old enough to hang out with them. She recalled one time in particular when about eight kids had squeezed into a booth here, and she'd ended up sitting next to Beau by accident. She could remember how he smelled, and how he'd put his arm behind her on the back of the booth to make more room, and how it had almost felt like he had his arm around her. She'd been so paralyzed with excitement, she hadn't been able to open her mouth all evening for fear her words would come out in a shriek.

Maybe it wasn't such a good idea to come here, she thought, knowing her face was now flushed, and knowing Beau would notice.

If he did, he said nothing. But she thought there was something knowing in the way he looked at her and almost smiled.

Had he suspected her monumental crush back then? She'd taken great pains to conceal it. Even now, she'd be mortified if he knew.

Aubrey wolfed down a cheeseburger and half an order of onion rings before she slowed down. "I guess terror builds up an appetite."

"You don't have to be afraid. I won't let anything happen to you."

Aubrey just shook her head. He had an inflated view of his abilities, she decided. A God complex. He decided who lived, who died, who went to jail and who got away. Or he thought he did. All it took was one punk with one gun to finish off either one of them.

But she could talk until she ran out of breath and he wouldn't get it.

"When did you become a bully?"

He laughed. "A what?"

"You just assume you'll get your way, that everyone will fall in with your wishes. And if someone doesn't see eye to eye with you, you push until they do."

He pulled back in surprise. "Where did *that* come from?"

"Taking that child from his mother. How do you know he wasn't better off there? His father probably has lots of money for lawyers and bounty hunters. He probably plays golf with the family court judge. If the mother turned around and offered you enough money, would you kidnap the kid back?"

He was suddenly not amused. "Understand this, Aubrey. First, Shelley is a prostitute and a drug addict. She was a neglectful, abusive mother and she had no business anywhere near a child. Second, I don't break the law. What I do is completely legal. I've had plenty of people try to hire me to snatch kids away from their legal guardians, and I turn them down flat. That would make me a criminal, and I'm not a criminal."

"You don't ever break the law?"

He thought about that for a few moments. "I won't go that far. Searching someone's desk without their permission is technically breaking the law. Exceeding the speed limit by a couple of miles is breaking the law. I doubt even you, Squeak, could claim you never broke the law."

She took a long sip of her iced tea. "I tried marijuana once."

Finally she earned a grin from Beau. "I dearly wish I could have seen that."

"But I only did it once."

"Once is all it takes, sometimes."

They both went silent, and Aubrey knew they were both thinking about Gavin. At his sentencing, he'd claimed once was all it took to get him hooked on crack. He'd been working undercover, and undercover cops were never supposed to use drugs. But he'd gotten into a bind, and if he hadn't smoked crack, the dealers he was infiltrating would have known he was a cop, and they'd have killed him. But once he crossed that line, it was easier the next time. And the next and the next. And then he had a habit, and stealing drugs from the evidence room had seemed like such an easy way to get a fix.

But Aubrey hadn't believed much of what went on at Gavin's sentencing. He'd worked some kind of deal with the prosecutor, and he said whatever they wanted him to say.

"Are you finished?" Beau said abruptly. "I'm gonna call Lori and see what she can come up with in the way of disguises."

BEAU LOOKED at his watch and silently cursed. He sat in Lori's living room, decked out in his most bad-ass clothes, which included his jeans and motorcycle boots, a muscle shirt with a black denim, studded vest and a do-rag on his head. Lori had added an earring and a huge fake tattoo on his arm of a skull and a bleeding rose.

It had taken little time to outfit him for a visit to Kink. But Aubrey was taking forever, and Beau had his doubts about whether he should have suggested she come with him to the S&M club. No matter what she wore, she would stand out as someone who didn't belong.

Lori emerged from the bedroom, smiling faintly. "She'll be out in a minute. She just has to put on the clothes."

"Did you give her a tattoo?"

"Three of them. And a couple of fake piercings, too." A faint rumbling in the distance caused both Lori and Beau to pause and listen. "Do you think that was thunder?"

"Probably."

She peeked out the curtains at the gathering dusk. "There are some dark clouds on the horizon. Maybe we'll finally get some rain." Texas wasn't officially in a drought, but rain was always welcome this time of year.

"It'll just get more humid if it rains."

"Pessimist."

The bedroom door cracked open. "Lori? I'm not sure this is right."

"Well, come on out and let's have a look."

The door opened slowly and Aubrey eased through it. At least, Beau *thought* it was Aubrey, though not even in his wildest fantasies had his childhood friend worn a leather bustier, a miniskirt, fishnet hose and thigh-high boots. A blue-green snake tattoo coiled around one slender arm; on the other was some kind of esoteric symbol, vaguely occult. He didn't even want to think about where the third tattoo might be.

A studded collar, a long black wig and generous makeup gave her a slightly Goth look, completing the image.

Beau whistled as his body responded viscerally.

This was one undercover job he was going to enjoy— pretending she was his plaything for the evening.

"I can't go out in public like this!" she almost wailed. "What if one of my students sees me? Or worse, one of my colleagues?"

"If your colleagues are hanging out at Kink," Beau pointed out, "they would hardly call attention to themselves. Anyway, your own mother wouldn't recognize you, so don't worry."

"You look fabulous," Lori said, adjusting the wig slightly. "Now hold your head up, throw your shoulders back, and look at every man you see as if they're worms. You definitely want to give them the idea you're the boss—not the other way around."

"Huh?"

"Aubrey, honey," Beau said, trying to sound deadly serious, "if you act submissive in this place, someone's liable to put you over their knee and spank you." He had to admit, the thought had already crossed his deviant mind. Was she wearing a garter belt?

Aubrey turned a pretty shade of pink, but her hands, now sporting long, red nails, bunched into fists. "They better not try it."

"Good," Lori said. "Keep that sneer in place. Hopefully the lights will be low, so no one will notice if you blush."

Aubrey raised a hand to her face self-consciously. Beau just grinned. "Ready, Squeak?"

"Do *not* call me that."

"No, ma'am, Mistress Aubrey. Sorry."

Aubrey made a strangled sound as they headed out the door.

Chapter Five

It was dark by the time Aubrey and Beau left for Kink. They'd considered stopping by Beau's house and getting his motorcycle, but Aubrey vetoed this idea.

"It's going to rain," she said confidently. She could smell it in the air, and the thunder, a distant suggestion of stormy weather a few minutes ago, was louder now. "Anyway, if I tried to ride a motorcycle in this skirt, we'd be arrested for indecent exposure before we even got to the club."

Beau conceded, and they took his car. But he parked it several blocks away, explaining that his souped-up black Mustang was distinctive enough that it might be noticed. If his presence were noted, it could put a damper on the free flow of information they were hoping for.

"Let me do the talking," he warned her. "Remember, you're there to make me look authentic so the other patrons will open up to me."

"I thought you said I was good at getting people to drop their guard."

"An insurance agent is a little different from the folks we're dealing with tonight. If you blow your cover with the wrong person, it could get ugly."

Aubrey thought Beau was exaggerating. Still, she would keep his warning in mind.

It was almost nine o'clock by the time they reached the front door of the club, which was up a flight of rickety stairs. The entrance was unassuming. All the windows were blackened, with only one small neon sign indicating this was a club at all. There were no beer signs or drink specials being touted to draw in patrons.

But apparently Kink didn't need more customers, Aubrey thought after Beau paid an exorbitant cover charge and they walked inside. The place was packed, even at this relatively early hour.

Aubrey remembered Lori's advice. She pushed her shoulders back and stuck her chest out, though she wasn't accustomed to showing off her own cleavage, which the silly bustier enhanced to a ridiculous degree. She assumed a haughty expression and walked with a confident gait.

Beau, on the other hand, just looked like Beau wearing a do-rag and sunglasses.

Aubrey had feared her extreme costume would make her stand out, but now she wondered if she should have gone even further. It almost seemed as if the S&M crowd competed to see who could have the most piercings or cover the most square inches of flesh with tattoos. Some of the costumes were ridiculous. One man wore a full suit of medieval armor. A woman was a dead ringer for Xena, Warrior Princess, and there were several gladiators in the crowd. Some merely looked rough-edged and grungy. But none looked like college professors. Beau was right—she probably would have created a panic if she'd entered as she'd been dressed earlier.

A young man wearing tights and—yes, a cod-piece—approached her. "Is my mistress accompanied this evening?" he asked, his eyes averted.

"Er…" Okay, what would a proper dominatrix say? "You're too pathetic to waste my spit on."

The young man dropped to his knees and cowered. "Oh, please, mistress, what have I done to earn your disfavor?"

"You were born." She stepped over him and headed for the bar. The stupid boots were already killing her feet, and she saw an empty barstool.

Beau was right behind her. "Are you sure you've never been in here before?" His voice held a grudging respect.

She decided not to answer. A slight air of mystery wouldn't hurt her reputation any. Squeak, indeed.

Beau ordered a beer for himself. "And the lady will have a—"

"Excuse me?" she interrupted disdainfully as she cocked one hip onto the barstool. She realized she was showing the top of one stocking and resisted the urge to pull down the hem of her skirt. "The lady can order for herself. She would like…" Not her usual white wine spritzer. "…a bloody Mary. And you, worm." She looked down her nose at Beau. "You may pay for it."

"I think you're enjoying this," Beau said under his breath as he pulled a wad of bills from his jeans pocket and peeled off a ten. "Just remember what we're here for."

His words blunted her momentary enjoyment. Someone in this bar might be the one who'd attacked her and threatened Patti, who was still missing. As of a few minutes ago, when Aubrey had checked her messages on the cell phone, Patti hadn't checked in.

Aubrey corralled her inner dominatrix and focused. She looked for any man who might have a wound on his right forearm, where she'd bitten her attacker. Almost all of the men went sleeveless, the better to display their bulging biceps, and she saw no suspiciously jagged cuts or bandages.

"You're new here," the bartender said as he placed her drink on the bar in front of her. He was a slight man, perhaps five-foot-eight, with curly blond hair and a soft, cherubic mouth that made him seem childlike. But there was nothing childlike about his costume. He wore cowboys' chaps—with no pants underneath, just a pair of tight red bikini underwear. And no shirt. But both his nipples were pierced with silver rings, and he wore wide straps of studded leather on both forearms.

"Just moved to Payton," she said, trying to find some place she could look that wouldn't be embarrassing. She settled for his eyes, which were a pale blue. "A friend told me about this place."

Beau stood beside her, tense, watching. She knew he wasn't happy about her chatting up the bartender. But what was she supposed to do? He'd asked her a direct question. To ignore him might arouse suspicion.

"Are you after any particular action?" the bartender asked.

"Not really. Just checking the place out. Though if something catches my eye…" She ran one red fingernail up Beau's muscular arm. His nostrils flared, but he remained silent.

"Yeah, well, a word to the wise," the bartender said. "You're not the only new face I see in here tonight. Better check with me before you go to the dungeons with any strangers.''

He gave Beau a meaningful look.

The dungeons? Aubrey had noticed a sign for ''Dungeons'' pointing down a staircase, but she'd thought it was just a clever way of pointing out the rest rooms.

Beau leaned close to whisper in her ear. ''The dungeons are private rooms where you can act out your fantasies away from prying eyes.''

A shiver crawled up Aubrey's spine. She could think of a few fantasies she'd like to act out with Beau, but they leaned more toward feathers and whipped cream than whips and chains. She shook off that unwelcome thought, though her face felt warm again. Thank goodness for the low lights.

Thunder boomed outside, rattling the liquor bottles behind the bars. ''Sounds like the storm is for real,'' she said to the bartender, wanting to prolong the conversation. But he'd turned away from her and was loading up the tray of a waitress who was, in fact, all but topless. She wore red leather shorts, which didn't completely cover her bottom, and the only thing covering her breasts were a pair of wide elastic suspenders. She didn't even blink when a drunk biker-looking guy snapped her back with one of the suspenders, then gave her rump a hard slap.

Had Patti actually worked in this place? Aubrey thought, less amused than she'd been a moment before. Had she let strange men grope her?

''So, who's the friend who sent you here?'' the bartender asked, suddenly attentive to her again.

Aubrey sipped her bloody Mary, which was so strong she almost winced. Beau had left her side, she noticed with some alarm. But then she spotted him only a few feet away, talking to an older man with a grizzled beard and an improbably huge beer belly peeking out from under a dirty T-shirt.

"Her name's Patti," Aubrey said. "I don't know her too well, but she said she worked here, or used to work here or something."

The bartender's pale blue eyes suddenly sparkled with interest. "Yeah? I know Patti. She used to be hot, till she had a baby. Then she got fat. Some of the guys here like that, I guess, 'cause she still makes the tips."

Fat? Patti? It was on the tip of Aubrey's tongue to argue that Patti had been an anorectic junkie before Sara. But she'd just said she didn't know Patti well. Her lies were going to trip her up if she wasn't careful. No wonder Beau hadn't wanted her to try to get information on her own.

Still, this guy knew Patti, which meant he might know to whom she owed money. She didn't want to discourage the flow of information.

"So where is Patti, anyway?" the bartender asked. The question had an edge to it, though the man was trying to act like it was no big deal. "I thought she was working tonight."

"She told me she quit. She's heading out west. San Francisco or someplace."

The bartender slammed down the glass he'd been washing. "When did she tell you this?"

"When I saw her. Yesterday, or maybe today. I lose track of time." Now she was getting into hot water, making up the lies as she went along. Her gaze flickered to the bartender's leather armbands. They could be covering a bite mark. Was it remotely possible that almost the first person she'd talked to in this club was her attacker?

No, she was being paranoid. He'd resumed washing glasses, but he kept a close watch on her. "Does she know someone in San Francisco?"

Aubrey shrugged and hopped off the bar stool. "I don't know. I met her at a Burger King and we talked for a few minutes. She didn't tell me her whole life story." She started to leave, but the bartender reached over the bar and grabbed her arm.

"Wait."

She wrenched her arm free. "What do you think you're doing, jerk-off?"

Just then a particularly loud boom of thunder rattled the whole building like an earthquake, and the lights went out. It was black as a cave. A few women squealed, but mostly there was nervous laughter.

"Group grope!" someone shouted.

A hand reached out and grasped Aubrey's breast, while another reached under her skirt and helped himself to a handful of her bottom.

"Hey!" she objected, lashing out with an elbow. The breast grabber pulled away with a gratifying *oof!* She kicked back with her sharp-heeled boot and managed to dislodge the cheek-fondler, just as another man pressed his face into her chest and tried to put his tongue down her cleavage.

"Ugh, disgusting!" she said as she pushed him away. "Beau? Beau, where are you?"

"Aubrey?" She heard him calling her name, but he wasn't close by. There was no way he'd find her in the dark in this crowd.

A hand clamped around her upper arm and dragged her determinedly away from the bar. She tried lashing out at her captor, but this one was stronger and far more determined than the others.

"Let me go, you filthy…slug-slime!" But the insult, which had worked so well on the codpiece man, had no effect on this brute, who seemed to be dragging her with a specific destination in mind.

Rape wasn't out of the question in a place like this. She screamed and fought in earnest, dropping to the floor, becoming dead weight. But her screams didn't elicit any help, as several other people were screaming melodramatically. And all dropping to the floor accomplished was to prompt her caveman to clamp one arm around her ribs and drag her backward. She could feel the leather band around his forearm. Either it was one of the gladiators, or the blond bartender.

She fought like a wildcat, but her captor had managed to pin one of her arms between their bodies and he was holding her other wrist, so she couldn't inflict any damage with her artificial nails. Her wig came off in the struggle, her real hair tumbling free from the pins Lori had tamed it with.

She felt herself being dragged down a flight of stairs and realized where they were heading—The Dungeons. In a private, locked, soundproof room, this Neanderthal could do anything he pleased with her.

She summoned her strength for one last scream. "Beau! Help me! I'm in The Dun—" A stinging blow to her head, right where she'd been hit earlier that day, stunned her to silence. By the time she had her wits about her again, she'd been shoved through another doorway. The door slammed shut behind her as she fell to what felt like a stone floor, and she prayed she'd be left alone. But no such luck. The horrible man was in here with her. She got up on her haunches, ready to grab his legs and take him down when he came near again. If she could just get him to lose his balance and fall on this stone floor, she might get lucky and he'd hurt himself.

She heard a match striking and turned in that direction. She saw the face of her attacker briefly illuminated—the bartender. He lit a torch mounted to the wall, and then a couple more. Now she could see she really was in a dungeonlike room, all lined with stone. All around the room were what looked like medieval torture devices—a rack, an egg-shaped cage hanging from a chain, for trapping someone's head, she imagined, several sizes of whips, and one dangerous-looking machine—she didn't even dare imagine how it worked.

There were several sets of manacles chained to the wall, too.

Was this, then, her fate? To be tortured to death? Her stomach roiled at the prospect. She could hardly stand to get a paper cut. The prospect of pain reduced her to quivering jelly. She knew she would tell this guy whatever he wanted to know, do whatever he asked of her to avoid a leather whip.

He walked over to stand beside her and look down at her. She couldn't make herself launch her body at his legs; she was paralyzed with terror, especially when she saw what he held in his hand—a small but wicked-looking whip made up of several narrow strands of leather.

He caressed the whip. "Stand up."

She scrambled to her feet.

"Go stand against the wall." When she didn't move fast enough, he struck lightning-quick with the small whip. It bit into her upper arm. She looked down at her arm, expecting blood, but there was just a faint red mark.

"It can do a lot worse," he said, his soft little mouth wearing an obscene smirk.

She moved to the wall. He manacled first one wrist, then the other, so that her arms were outstretched. But he left her feet free.

That's your mistake, you jerk.

"Now," he said in a deceptively patient voice, "tell me everything you know about Patti."

Instead she kicked forward, catching him right in his red bikini underwear. He crumpled to the floor in a howl of pain, and Aubrey felt the exhilaration of triumph. Only moments earlier she'd imagined she would be a sniveling coward, but from somewhere she'd found the courage to strike back.

It was a short-lived victory.

"That," he said when he could speak, "will cost you."

The whip snaked out again and caught her on the thigh. It stung like a burn, even through her stocking. Her eyes watered, but Aubrey forced herself not to cry out. She wouldn't give this toad the satisfaction.

BEAU HAD HEARD Aubrey's scream, and he'd worked his way toward it. But in this half-panicked, writhing crowd, the going wasn't easy. Then he'd heard Aubrey call out his name, from a different direction, and he realized he'd made no progress at all.

She'd sounded like she was in trouble, too. He cursed himself for bringing her here. He should have insisted he could do this alone. And he could have—he'd already gotten some information that would help.

The lights came back on. Some people cheered,

some booed. Beau frantically searched the room for some sign of Aubrey, but he saw nothing.

Then he spotted a black wig lying on the floor. He picked it up and examined it. It was Aubrey's, all right. Her scent clung to it.

He was standing right by the staircase that went down to The Dungeons. That must have been where Aubrey was taken. He headed that way, but a shirtless man in a centurion helmet holding an ax barred his way. "Can't go down there. It costs extra."

The centurion was huge, probably three hundred pounds. Even in his desperation to find Aubrey, Beau wasn't crazy enough to think he could get the best of this guy.

"How much?" Beau demanded, reaching into his pocket for more money.

"Fifty. Where's your partner?"

"Partner?"

"You can't go down there alone. That don't make no sense."

Beau looked around wildly. His gaze fell on a blue-eyed Viking woman with blond hair down to her waist, bull's-eye breastplates and a helmet with horns. She looked back with obvious interest.

He grabbed her by the arm. "Come downstairs with me."

"Sure, but I'm not submissive."

"No, I don't imagine so." He paid the fee. The centurion informed him he was assigned to room one.

"Oooh, that's my favorite," the Viking cooed to Beau. "Want to be my galley slave?"

He ignored her. When he reached the bottom of the stairs, he found a hallway with four doors. He skipped room one, since he assumed it would be empty. He pushed open the door to room two, which was decked out like a sultan's harem, with bright silk hangings and pillows on the floor, middle-eastern carpets and a gurgling fountain.

"This isn't our room," the blonde said, pouting.

Beau pulled out of that room and went for room three. Inside he found a redhead in a French maid's outfit bent over the knee of a guy dressed like a butler. The woman screamed.

"What do you think you're doing?" the butler howled in protest.

"Try locking the door," Beau said as he withdrew.

"You are some kind of crazy," the Viking said, half admiring, half alarmed. "We're in one, room one!"

Beau went for the last room, number four. It was locked. Beau beat on it with his fist. "Open up! Police!" Strictly speaking, it was against the law for him to impersonate an officer. But right now he didn't care. He'd do whatever it took to get that door open and get to Aubrey before she was seriously hurt.

"Do these rooms have any other way out?" he asked the Viking, since she seemed to be familiar with the place.

"No, each only has one door. Are you really a cop?" she asked, sounding intrigued.

"I used to be."

"Want to interrogate me? For you, I think I *could* be submissive."

"Oh, for crying out loud." Beating on the door produced no results, so he grabbed what looked like a medieval executioner's ax from the wall and proceeded to tear the door down. The blade wasn't very sharp; the ax had of course been intended for display, not practical use. Still, it did chew through the wood.

He aimed blow after blow near the latch until the wood around it collapsed. Finally, with a couple of slams with his shoulder, he crashed through.

What he saw brought his heart up into his throat. Aubrey was cuffed spread-eagle to the stone wall. Her arms and legs were marred with angry red stripes.

"Watch out!" she called, just as a man launched himself at Beau from behind the door. The Viking screamed. Beau fell, but he grabbed a handful of leather as he did. The chaps came off in his hand, and Aubrey's captor, wearing only a pair of red underwear, was out the door in a flash.

Beau's instincts told him to chase the guy down. How far could he get in that half-naked state? But his concern for Aubrey won out, and he went for her instead. She didn't look as if she was in mortal danger, but she must be terrified.

He cupped her face in his hands and looked into her eyes. "Aubrey. Honey, are you all right?"

"Never mind me! Go after him!"

But Beau didn't listen. He freed her from the manacles, which fortunately were like the play handcuffs he'd had as a child, requiring only the flip of a lever to get them open.

As soon as she was free, he held her against him. "Did he hurt you?"

"Not badly. We should go after him." But then she crumpled against him and sobbed.

"I'm not going anywhere." He stroked her hair. "I'm so sorry, Aubrey. I did a lousy job of protecting you. I shouldn't have let you come here in the first place."

"I'm okay," she said, getting herself under control. "Just more scared than anything. She pulled away.

"Look, his silly little whip didn't even break the skin."

"Just who exactly is this?" the Viking demanded. "I don't go for threesomes, you know."

Chapter Six

"We can't go to the police, not when we were in an S&M club dressed for action," Beau reasoned. They were walking back to his car, the rain soaking them through. But Aubrey didn't care. It was a warm rain, and it felt cleansing, like a shower. She wanted to wash the bartender's touch off her skin as soon as possible. Unfortunately, she couldn't wash the memories away.

"I don't want to go to the cops," she said, picturing Lyle Palmer's disapproving face as he made her go blow-by-blow through the whole humiliating event. "Let's just get away from here." Aubrey was still shaking, and her skin stung in dozens of places now that her adrenaline was seeping away. "I suppose technically I couldn't prove a crime was committed anyway. Just walking into a place like that could be construed as asking for what I got."

Beau just growled. They'd reached his car, and he unlocked the door with a button on his key chain. But he gallantly helped her into the passenger seat, making sure she was settled before he closed the door.

She hadn't expected him to be so fiercely protective of her. His tenderness, and the way he'd caressed her hair and called her "honey," stuck with her far more emphatically than the bartender's less gentle ministrations.

"His name's Cory Silvan," Beau said. "He's a part-time bartender, full-time drug dealer. He deals mostly with meth-amphetamines."

"You're kidding. That was Patti's drug of choice. How'd you find that out?"

"That old guy I was talking to? Former cop."

"The one with the huge belly?"

"Cops have some strange predilections, just like every other group. He's a regular at Kink. Says he mostly just likes to watch. But he's had his eye on Cory. Cory's got that innocent face, and he's in good with the college crowd. Likes to give away free samples and get them hooked."

Aubrey shivered. That was exactly how Patti had gotten started.

"Want me to turn on the heater?" he asked.

"No, that's okay." Then she blurted out, "Thank you for saving me. I'm sorry I didn't listen to you and keep my mouth shut. But the bartender—Cory—kept me talking, and I guess before I knew it, I was the one revealing information instead of him. All I learned was that Patti was still working there and that she earned good tips."

"Which she turned over to Cory. She owed him thirteen thousand dollars."

"What?"

"She's a heavy user."

"No, Beau, that's not true. I saw what Patti was like when she was using. Skinny, hollow eyes, sallow skin. She's healthy now."

Beau didn't argue further, but Aubrey could tell he

didn't believe her. "Maybe the debt's an old one," he finally conceded. "Anyway, apparently she'd disappeared from the scene, and he lost track of her. He wasn't happy about being stiffed. But then he found her, and he threatened her somehow if she didn't go back to work at Kink and pay him back."

It somehow made Aubrey feel better to know Patti wasn't willingly working as a sex-club waitress.

"So what now?" she asked.

"Right now we take care of you."

"I'm fine, now, really. You don't have to worry about me, I'm tougher than I look." Never mind that she was still shivering inside from fear and revulsion.

Beau was quiet for a long time. Finally he said, "You've been assaulted twice today. Either time, you could have been killed. I'm not willing to see you in that kind of danger again. So we're gonna rethink this whole thing."

"And where are we going to do that?"

"My house. It's the only place I'm sure you'll be safe."

Beau's house. "Oh, I don't think—"

"It's not up for discussion. If you want my help, you follow my rules."

Oh, how she hated that macho attitude. If she was really brave, she would tell him to stuff it, that she could handle this on her own, that he was overreacting to the danger. But she was too damn scared. So she let Beau drive her to his house. Her only hope was that it would be cleaner than the First Strike office.

Aubrey was surprised when Beau turned the car onto a road leading into Skylark Meadow, one of Payton's nicer neighborhoods. The subdivision had been built in the '70s in a wooded, hilly area, and the builders had taken great pains to preserve as many trees as possible. It quickly became the trendy place to live. Many of the University bigwigs had settled here, and the property values were among the highest in town.

After winding through streets with picturesque names like Yellow Finch Lane and Swansong Place, Beau pulled the Mustang into a driveway of a large, modern-looking house built on the side of a hill. A wrought-iron fence surrounded it, and the front yard was landscaped with huge rocks and ground cover, probably requiring minimum upkeep.

He reached across her and pulled a garage opener from his glove box. But it wasn't an ordinary one. He had to push in a numerical code to get it to work. Suddenly the house appeared more like a fortress to her, perched on its hill.

"You live here?" she asked, unable to keep the shocked tone out of her voice.

"What were you expecting?"

"I don't know. But not this. I guess the bounty hunter business is pretty profitable."

"On average, not really. I got lucky once. A billionaire paid me handsomely to bring back his runaway teenage daughter. That reward bought this house."

"How much did you make off my brother?"

Beau's expression was pained. "Aubrey, don't go there. Not tonight. I'm tired, I'm hurt, you're hurt—"

"You're hurt?" She immediately felt contrite. She hadn't even considered the fact that he might have gotten injured trying to rescue her. He just seemed so invincible. But he'd taken a tumble on that hard stone floor. She had her own bruises proving how uncomfortable that was.

"Nothing a soak in the hot tub won't fix."

The thought of Beau naked in a hot tub wasn't an image she wanted to focus on right now.

The inside of the house was dramatic and very…male, starting with a monochromatic kitchen—gray, black and white—that looked as if it had never been used. Moving into the living room, there wasn't a soft color anywhere. Everything was black, white or brown, and the furniture was leather—all of it. She could smell the leather. Kind of like new-car smell, only better.

And it was clean. No stray beer bottles or laundry or old pizza cartons.

Floor-to-ceiling windows overlooked a creek, dramatically illuminated with landscape lighting. Aubrey realized it would take a grappling hook for anyone to approach the house from the back.

Beau stopped in the middle of the living room and whistled softly. A scrambling sound followed—a dog getting to its feet? That was a surprise.

A big dog, Aubrey amended, her heart in her throat, as an enormous Rottweiler trotted down the stairs and straight to Beau.

"Oh, my God."

"This is Sophie," Beau said, scratching the dog behind its ears. He pointed to Aubrey. "Friend."

The dog stared at Aubrey for a moment, then trotted over to sniff her. Aubrey stood stock-still. "Does she bite?"

"She'll be nice to you, now that I've informed her you're one of the good guys. But she's trained to attack."

"Oh, Lord."

"It's okay. You can pet her."

Aubrey declined. The dog sniffed her up and down, then, apparently not satisfied, stuck its nose under her skirt.

Aubrey stepped away. "Hey!"

"Sophie, no," Beau said in a quiet but authoritative voice. "Go lie down."

The dog immediately obeyed, plodding over to a rug by the fireplace and plopping down.

"Guess you don't need a security system with her around," Aubrey said.

"I have both. It would take an army to get into this place. You can sleep soundly here."

Aubrey doubted that. "Oh, Beau, you're bleeding." He had a huge gash on his left arm. She hadn't noticed it in the car because it was facing away from her. "Do you have something to put on that?"

Beau looked at the cut without much concern at first. Then he frowned. His arm was covered in dried blood, and the cut was still oozing. "Damn, I hope I didn't bleed all over my car. I guess it wouldn't hurt to clean that up a bit."

"Stitches probably wouldn't hurt, either."

"Come on, it's not that bad. But I could probably use some help patching myself up." He left her duffel bag at the bottom of the stairs, then led her down a hallway where she assumed the master bedroom was. She had a few qualms about joining Beau anywhere near a bed, but she supposed they were both a bit too battered and exhausted to care about sex.

His bedroom was huge, dominated by a king-size bed. The bed had been made up, more or less, with a fluffy down comforter smoothed over the top. She'd never known a guy who made his own bed. Which led her to wonder if he'd had overnight company recently.

The thought was highly displeasing.

The master bath was done in blinding-white tile with black accents. Lots of fluffy black and red towels hung on the racks. One was on the floor, and the single concession to male untidiness was almost comforting.

There was, indeed, a big square tub with whirlpool jets. She couldn't help but picture Beau there. She quickly looked away.

Beau stuck his arm in the sink and ran warm water over it, then soaped it up with liquid antibacterial soap. "It's not that bad. Couple of butterfly bandages should take care of it." He smeared some antibacterial cream on it, then rummaged through a drawer until he found a box of the bandages he wanted.

He handed them to Aubrey. "Here you go, nurse."

She had second thoughts about agreeing to bandage him up. He seemed to be handling the first-aid work fine on his own. But if she backed out now, he would know she didn't want to touch him. She wished she'd changed her clothes first. The silly leather bustier and short skirt suddenly felt more indecent than before.

She opened the box of bandages with nervous hands and selected three butterflies. Beau sat on a stool and held out his arm, watching her closely. Her mouth was dry.

"So how much did you make off my brother?" she asked, deliberately stirring up the one subject that was sure to keep them angry at each other.

"Aubrey..."

"No, I want to know."

Beau sighed. "His bond was a hundred thousand dollars. I got ten percent."

"Ten thousand dollars. It seems like a lot of money, but when you compare it to the value of a lifelong friendship—"

"The money had nothing to do with it," Beau said, his voice dangerously soft. "I brought him in *because* he was my friend."

"You don't shoot friends in the leg."

"You do if you don't want to kill them."

"You should have let him go. You know what they do to cops in prison."

"He'd have never gotten away, Aubrey. Every cop in the city was looking for him, not to mention the FBI. And if the wrong cop found him, he'd have been dead—even if he didn't shoot first."

"What do you mean? Are you saying Gavin shot at you?"

"Look, just forget it, okay?"

"No, I won't forget it. I heard your testimony in court. You said you saw he had a gun and you shot first. Now, are you trying to tell me that's not true?"

He remained stubbornly silent, but she could tell by the set of his mouth, and the muscles working in his jaw, that she'd infuriated him.

Beau literally had to bite his tongue to keep his temper from boiling over. Aubrey had a real blind spot where Gavin was concerned. She would never believe her precious older brother had done the things he'd been accused of. And she would never in a million years believe that Gavin, half-insane with desperation and cornered in an abandoned barn, had fired the first shot.

He hadn't intended to kill Beau, but the shot had come too close for Beau to take any chances. A much better marksman than Gavin, Beau had hit what he aimed for, quickly putting an end to the standoff.

Aubrey's hands were gentle as she squeezed the cut on Beau's arm closed and applied the butterfly bandage. But her words were like a dull stick poking an old wound.

"The firearms expert said his weapon hadn't been fired," she said smugly.

"Yeah, but the idiots who arrested him didn't swab his hand, did they?" If they had, they'd have found gunpowder residue, and an inconsistency Beau would have found hard to explain. But he'd been counting on some incompetence, and he'd lucked out.

"What are you talking about?" Aubrey asked impatiently.

"Nothing. Forget it."

"I want to know!"

"Why? You've already made up your mind. I'm the bad guy, Gavin is the misguided scapegoat. Nothing I could say would change your opinion, so why should I bother?" He suddenly realized he was on his feet, that his hands were gripping Aubrey's upper arms. He'd stopped himself just short of shaking her.

Her eyes filled with tears as she looked up at him. "Because I don't want you to be the bad guy."

The next thing he knew he was kissing her, and his hands were all over her, and hers were on him, sliding under his shirt, raking him lightly with those long red nails. And he had one hand on her bottom, and the leather felt so sexy and she smelled so good. Though her hair still held a trace of cigarette smoke from the bar there was something better underneath it, like vanilla and cinnamon, yeah, cinnamon, and her mouth was hot and wet and ripe, and he could just imagine what it might feel like if she kissed him *there* and *there*...

His hand wandered beneath her skirt, and his runaway fantasy came to a screeching halt. She wore cotton panties. Not that cotton panties were a turn-off. He'd seen them in the Victoria's Secret catalogue, so it wasn't that. It was the reminder that this hot babe in leather wasn't real. This was Aubrey, his best friend's little sister, who wore wholesome cotton underthings.

He stopped abruptly and pulled his mouth from hers. Moved his hand to her back. Pushed her gently away from him.

"What?" she almost shrieked, and he recognized that the need they'd kindled without meaning to was as strong in her as in him.

"If you don't get out of here in about five seconds, we are both going to be very, very sorry."

She stiffened, and he was already sorry. He never should have let this happen. Aubrey wasn't a woman to ravish on the bathroom floor. She was all that was good and honest and sweet that had ever been a part of his life, and he'd been about to ruin that. Yeah, he wanted her, but it was the kind of desire that ought not to be indulged.

"Where do you want me to sleep?" she said, chin up, defiant in the face of his rejection.

"Pick any of the rooms upstairs."

She stared at him a moment longer, and he prayed she wouldn't push it. His willpower was only so strong. He turned away from her, reached into the drawer where he'd found the bandages and pulled out a jar of burn salve. He handed it to her.

"This should help those whip stings."

She took it and walked out of the bathroom without a backward look.

AUBREY DIDN'T HAVE a prayer of getting a good night's sleep. Even after a warm shower, even after applying the soothing salve to the pink stripes on her skin and slipping on a soft cotton nightshirt, even after climbing under the covers of the soft bed in the room she'd chosen and listening to the rain patter on the roof, she could hardly bring herself to close her eyes.

Her thoughts whirled in her head like leaves chasing each other in the wind. Patti and Sara, still missing…the assault at her house…Cory, the drug dealer, threatening to kill her if she didn't tell him where Patti was. All of today's unsettling events were mixed up with the mental image she'd built of Beau shooting Gavin, of how it must have happened, based on the evidence and testimony she'd heard in court two years ago.

And wondering, What had Beau meant when he pointed out that the police hadn't swabbed Gavin's hand? Granted, it was an oversight. But what difference did it make, if his gun hadn't been discharged?

She must have finally slept, because the sun woke her up. Last night's storm had blown over, leaving the world outside looking pristine and cool. That would last about ten minutes, she figured, until the summer heat turned Payton into a steam bath.

The first thing Aubrey did was check her cell phone for messages, and she had one. She'd left the phone on all night, in case Patti tried to call, but apparently she hadn't heard it ring. She dialed in to get the message, praying it would be Patti.

Instead she heard Lyle Palmer's voice, low and serious.

"Aubrey, please call me as soon as possible." Nothing else but his phone number. The call had come in at 6:42, less than an hour ago. Early for Lyle to be at work. She called him back, her hands shaking.

This wasn't good news. She was sure of it. Had he heard about the debacle at Kink?

"Aubrey, good. Are you all right? You weren't at home. I was hoping you'd gone to stay with a friend, like I advised."

"Yes, I did."

"I need to meet with you. Where are you?"

She wasn't about to tell him she'd spent the night at Beau's house. "I can come to the station. But what's this about? Have you found Patti?"

He waited a fraction of a second too long before answering. "I really don't want to go into it over the phone."

Oh, God. She suddenly had a very, very bad feeling. Her rubbery legs refused to hold her up any longer, and she sank onto the bed. "Just tell me now. It's Patti, isn't it?"

"I'd really rather—"

"Just tell me! Is she dead?"

"She…I'm so sorry, Aubrey. She was found at a roadside rest stop, just outside of town. She apparently killed herself."

"How?" Aubrey made herself ask.

"Asphyxiation, with the car exhaust. It's a relatively painless way to—"

"Oh, my God. Sara. The baby. She didn't—"

"The baby wasn't with her. She probably left her with someone. Who would she trust with her baby?"

The only person Aubrey could think of was herself. "I don't know." This was too much. It was too awful. Aubrey struggled to hold herself together when all she wanted to do was fall to the carpet in a heap of despair.

"Does she have any other family in town?"

"Her father and brother. But she wouldn't—she's estranged from them. Lyle, this can't be right. Patti wouldn't kill herself."

"From everything you've told me, she was in some kind of trouble. Maybe it got to be too much for her to handle."

Aubrey couldn't envision Patti ending her own life, under any circumstances. "She would have left the baby with me. Oh, God, what if someone killed her and took the baby?"

"We'll do everything we can to find Sara," Lyle said soothingly.

"Let me break the news to her father and brother first, please," she said. "My uncle is ill. I'm afraid the shock of cops coming to his door might..."

"All right. Why don't you call me back when you've done that? Meanwhile, I'll put out a bulletin on the baby. Patti was holding a picture of her when she died. We can use that."

They ended the call, and Aubrey felt suddenly, achingly alone. She had to talk to someone, and Beau was the closest. That was her rationale as she headed down the stairs in her nightshirt, caving in to a need for the comfort of his arms, so primitive she couldn't even put a name to it.

The living room and kitchen were still dark, so she headed down the hall to his bedroom. She tapped lightly on the door. "Beau? Are you awake?" When she got no response she knocked harder, then opened the door a crack. His bed was empty, but looked as if it had been slept in.

She heard water running in the bathroom. She stepped inside the bedroom and headed that way.

GET SOME SLEEP. What had he been thinking? The whole night, all Beau could think about was Aubrey's warm, slender body lying in bed somewhere on the floor above him.

He hadn't expected to feel such strong, unrelenting desire for her.

At 6:00 a.m., he'd given up pretending to sleep. He felt marginally better after a shower. His shoulder was bruised black and blue from trying to bash the dungeon door down, and his muscles ached from swinging the dull ax. At least the cut didn't hurt much.

He'd just made his first stroke across his jaw with the razor when the bathroom door opened. He jumped, cut himself, reached for a weapon that wasn't there.

Aubrey yelped in surprise, then just stood there. She wore only a pale blue nightshirt that revealed most of her bare legs.

He recovered quickly. "Good morning," he said with a slow smile. He could have been a gentleman and averted his gaze when her nipples hardened beneath the tissue-thin nightshirt, but he'd always wanted to see Aubrey's breasts.

Finally the catatonia that had frozen her lifted. "I— I'm sorry," she said, backing out of the room. "I knocked, but I guess you didn't hear me." With that she closed the door.

Finally it registered with Beau what was wrong with this picture. Her face had been damp—with tears? He turned off the water, wrapped a towel around his hips, and left the bathroom. "Aubrey?"

She was sitting on the edge of his bed, her face pale, her curly hair an untidy reddish-brown cloud around her head. Her back was stiff, her hands clenched in her lap.

And yes, she was crying. She'd always had this uncanny way of weeping without making any noise, even when she'd been a child. She looked up at him with her huge green eyes, wet with tears.

"Patti's dead. I just talked to Lyle Palmer."

"Oh, Aubrey…" He didn't know what to say. So he sat down and put his arms around her and let her cry it out. Women's tears were one of the few things that could render him helpless. He had no idea what to say or do in the face of Aubrey's raw grief.

She didn't indulge long in her tears, just a couple of minutes. Then her breath came more evenly, and she sniffed a couple of times. "I've gotten you all wet."

He rubbed her back, refusing to let her go. "It's okay. I'm not made of sugar. You're going to be all right. Everything will be fine." Stupid words of comfort, really. But he couldn't think of anything else to say. He hated to see her hurting like this.

"How can you be so nice to me," she said against his shoulder, "when I was so mean to you last night?"

"Shh. Never mind about that."

But she pulled away and looked him in the face. "No, really. I should explain."

"You're like a terrier with a bone, you know that? No explanation is necessary." Besides, he had a pretty good idea what was going on with her last night.

"I was trying really hard to stay mad at you. Because after you rescued me like some knight in shining armor—''

''Aubrey, really.''

''All I could think about was kissing you. And there was your bed and that hot tub, and I was touching you and I was wearing those sexy clothes—''

''You *really* don't have to explain this, honey. I understand.'' And he didn't want to think about Aubrey in a leather miniskirt and a garter belt right now. He was already aroused, and with just a towel between him and the rest of the world, Aubrey would soon know it.

''I was just trying to find a way to keep you at a distance.''

''It didn't exactly work, did it?''

''Why did we stop?''

Why are you talking about this now? he wanted to ask. She'd just found out her cousin was dead. But he knew from his cop days that people reacted in all kinds of strange ways when a loved one died suddenly. They cried, they laughed, they went into denial, they avoided the subject, they took off running, they hid in closets, they got violent. There was no such thing as a typical reaction.

''We stopped because I was angry,'' he said. ''And I didn't want to make love with you the first time when I was still angry. That's not the right way to do it.''

''But you wanted to?''

''What do you think?''

That was all she needed to hear. She closed her eyes and pressed her lips to his.

He knew this wasn't right. Aubrey was a little bit out of her head right now. He marshaled every bit of willpower within reach and broke the kiss.

"Aubrey, honey, you're not thinking straight."

"Yes, I am," she said emphatically. "I'm not insane with grief or anything. And I'm not trying to lose myself in sex or dull my senses or escape, or reaffirm life or anything dumb like that. I just suddenly realized that life is too short and too uncertain to let stupid misunderstandings get in the way of our connections with each other.

"I could have died yesterday, not once but twice. I don't want to die without knowing what it feels like to make love with you."

Some part of Beau wanted to argue with her. Despite her protestations, she *was* trying to reaffirm life. He'd seen it before. He'd once had to inform a young wife that her husband had died in a traffic accident. Her reaction had been very similar to Aubrey's. He'd gently turned her down, of course, and later she'd apologized and thanked him for being a gentleman.

But he wasn't feeling nearly as gentlemanly with Aubrey. The realization that she'd been attracted to him all this time, just as he was to her, bowled him over. Maybe they shouldn't waste any more time.

He could rationalize it all he wanted, but the truth was, he was incapable of walking away. Aubrey stared solemnly at him, waiting for him to make a decision. Push her away? Or kiss her?

He kissed her.

Chapter Seven

Aubrey knew full well what she was doing as she wrapped her arms around Beau and kissed him with every ounce of longing she'd saved up over all those years she'd wanted him but couldn't have him. She was crossing a line, across which she could never retreat.

But hearing the news of Patti's death had done something to her. All the caution she'd cultivated throughout her whole life went right out the window. She'd meant what she'd said to Beau. Life *was* short, and so uncertain. She was simply no longer compelled to guard her heart so carefully.

Guard it for what? So she wouldn't get hurt? Oh, poor baby. Her beautiful cousin was lying on a cold slab at the morgue. *That* was something to fear. A few emotional bruises were nothing by comparison.

Beau fell back onto the bed, taking her with him. She twisted to a more comfortable position, throwing her leg across him. The towel he'd wrapped around his hips for modesty got bunched under her, somehow, so she yanked it free and threw it on the floor.

Beau pulled her nightshirt up to bare her midriff and breasts, so she could lie across him, hot skin to hot skin. His arousal pressed against her belly. She wiggled against him and rubbed back and forth, needing to experience the texture of his skin, the roughness of his chest hair against her sensitized nipples. That earned her a groan from Beau. He placed his hands on either side of her head and kissed her, hard, his fingers tangling in her tousled curls.

The sensory overload was almost too much. Her core felt as though it was about to have a serious meltdown. She didn't want any teasing or gentle caresses or soft sighs. She wanted mutual possession, and she wanted it now before the chance somehow slipped away from her.

Beau turned his head to the side, breaking the kiss. "Um, Aubrey..."

"I'm not going to allow you to be sensible," she said, breathing hard. "I know the timing is bad. But damn it, Beau, I need this. I need something to hold on to over the next few days. It doesn't have to mean anything. I'm not a clinging vine, and I won't try to turn this into something it's not. But—"

"Hey, take it easy." He cupped her face in one hand, gently, and she realized maybe soft caresses *were* part of what she needed. "I was only going to ask you if you want me to do something about protection."

"Oh. Yes. Good. Good idea."

She raised up to let him scoot out from underneath her, taking the opportunity to appreciate what a splendid body he had. The muscles in his broad back stretched and slithered over one another as he reached into the drawer of the nightstand. Then she noticed the terrible bruise on his shoulder.

"My God, Beau. Your shoulder..."

He closed the drawer and leaned back on the pillows. "It's just a bruise."

"It's the biggest bruise I've ever seen."

"That's what I get for using my body as a battering ram."

"Oh, Beau." She kissed him again, harder, her desire blossoming as she remembered what he'd gone through to rescue her last night.

That was the last they talked for a long while. Aubrey stopped kissing him long enough to draw the nightshirt over her head and toss it aside. She was naked underneath. She draped herself atop him once again, reveling in the feel of his erection pressed against the tender flesh of her inner thigh.

Beau squeezed her bottom, pressing her against his hardness, and he groaned each time she thrust her pelvis against him, instinctively mimicking the dance of sex.

She suspected he was holding back for her, but in truth she was ready. She didn't want to count the years she'd waited for this moment, she just wanted it to happen. She grabbed the plastic packet out of his hand and ripped it open with her teeth.

"Do this," she ordered him. Her hands were shaking, and she assumed he'd had more practice at it than she had. He obliged her, accomplishing the task of sheathing himself efficiently, no fumbling.

As soon as he was ready, he rolled her over and nudged her legs open. "Like this?"

"Like, any way you want it." Just now, please. She hoped he wouldn't make her beg, but she was about to.

He didn't disappoint her. He entered her in one swift, smooth motion. The sensation of fullness was so pleasant, so unexpectedly blissful, that she had to close her eyes and savor it.

Beau placed his elbows on either side of her and kissed her at her temple, smoothing her hair out of her face. "Okay?"

She opened her mouth to tell him it was more than okay, that she'd never felt anything as fabulous as Beau Maddox inside her. How had she lived twenty-eight years without it? But no words came out of her mouth. Instead she squeaked.

"Aubrey?"

"Ah, yeah," was all she managed.

He began moving, slowly at first, creating a friction so exquisite Aubrey thought she might expire from it. The rhythm quickly accelerated. She heard a scream, not quite believing she'd made it herself. And then the world exploded.

"Aubrey, oh, Aubrey, honey…"

It felt as though she'd blacked out for a moment. When she came back to reality, she felt bathed in an incredible sense of rightness. Not quite contentment, because she knew in the back of her mind that Patti was still dead and Sara still missing. But somehow she knew now that she could get through the day.

Beau was now lying beside her, holding her softly, playing with a strand of her hair. "That was as good as I ever imagined it would be. And I have a pretty good imagination."

Somehow she managed a smile. "Thank you. For indulging me, I mean. I know it seems crazy, to have sex when I just found out—"

"It's normal."

With some effort, she dragged her mind back to the

real world. "We have to get moving. I promised Lyle I'd go to Uncle Wayne's and break the news."

"I'll come with you."

"You don't have to. If you could just take me back to my car—"

"Don't be ridiculous. I'm not letting you out of my sight."

Yesterday she would have bristled at his bossy tone. Today she just sighed, liking the proprietary note in his voice. For a little while, at least, she wanted to indulge in the naive fantasy that he actually cared for her, that they might somehow get past the fact that he was a lawless bounty hunter who'd shot her brother, and that this crazy act of passion she'd practically forced on him might lead to something more.

THOUGH IT HAD BEEN years since Beau had set foot on the Clarendon estate, he knew the way by heart. He was surprised, however, to find a set of cast-iron gates blocking the driveway. The gates had always been there, he supposed, but he couldn't recall anyone ever closing them. The security keypad and intercom were new, too.

He pulled up to the keypad and pushed the intercom button, then let Aubrey do the talking. She leaned across him to get closer to the microphone. He could smell his shampoo in her hair, and it drove him wild. He had to stop himself from touching the soft reddish curls, still slightly damp from her shower. He had no idea whether she would continue to welcome physical intimacy from him, or whether this morning was a onetime deal. The circumstances were so odd, he had no way of knowing. He knew what *he* wanted—to get her back in bed as soon as possible. But he might not be thinking straight.

"David? Is that you?" Aubrey asked when a male voice came over the speaker, asking in a friendly tone who was there. "It's me, Aubrey."

"Aubrey!" David sounded very pleased. The gates immediately opened.

Beau drove through, then up the long driveway around a huge fountain toward the limestone mansion. He'd forgotten how huge this place was, but it was definitely one of the biggest estates in Payton. Wayne Clarendon was old money. His grandfather had been one of Payton's first mayors.

"Would you mind if I dropped you off?" Beau asked.

"Gee, what happened to 'I'm not letting you out of my sight'?"

"You should be safe enough here, with the security gates and all. There are bars on the windows, too." On both floors, everything but the attic. When had Wayne Clarendon become paranoid? "I have something I need to do." What he really needed to do was dump a couple of his cases on Rex Bettencourt, the other bounty hunter who worked at First Strike. Protecting Aubrey had just become his full-time job. Ace probably wouldn't be happy about his new gig, since there was no money in it, but that was tough. One of the things he loved about being a bounty hunter was being able to pick and choose his cases. He wasn't hurting for money, especially not with the reward money for the Langford kid he'd soon be receiving.

"You're going after her, aren't you?" Aubrey asked anxiously.

"You mean Sara?"

Aubrey nodded. "You're the best at tracking down fugitives and missing persons—everyone says so. If anyone can find Sara, you can."

"Um, no, I wasn't planning to go after Sara." He couldn't protect Aubrey and search for Sara at the same time. "Look, much as I despise Lyle Palmer, this time I think he's right. Patti stashed Sara someplace she thought would be safe." Aubrey had filled him in on the details as they'd driven over. "Now, maybe it's not someplace you or I would think of, and it might take a while to figure it out. She obviously wasn't thinking clearly. But Sara will probably turn up in the next few hours, as soon as news of Patti's death gets out."

"Would it hurt to start looking for her now anyway?"

"I'm sure the police are doing what they can. They've got more personnel and more resources than I do. Besides, if I got involved, Lyle would say I'm interfering with a police investigation. He'd love nothing better than to throw my butt in jail."

Aubrey studied him through narrowed eyes. "Okay."

Something was wrong with her sudden agreement. "Look, I'll talk to Craig, okay? I'll make sure everything's being done that should be done." Craig was his former partner on the force, and one of the few cops in this town that he trusted implicitly.

"Okay," Aubrey said again as he pulled to a stop in front of the mansion.

"I'll come back in a couple of hours."

"Don't bother."

"Okay, what did I do wrong?"

She didn't answer. Impulsively he leaned over to

peck her on the cheek. She ducked away from him before his lips could make contact and climbed out of the car as if it were on fire. She slammed the door and didn't give him a backward glance as she headed for the columned porch that sheltered the mansion's front entrance.

"Well, hell," he muttered. He'd been hoping her attitude toward him had softened after their incredible lovemaking this morning. Then he realized how foolish a hope that was. He and Aubrey had had sex—a simple release of tension that had done them both a world of good. Beyond that, he couldn't say, but it appeared he was definitely in the doghouse again.

AUBREY SHOOK OFF her anger at Beau and focused on the upcoming meeting with her relatives. Again she berated herself for not staying in better touch with them. It was terrible that a tragedy brought them together now.

David opened the door before Aubrey could knock, welcoming her with the boyish smile and twinkling blue eyes that made him look younger than his true age, which was the same as hers. He wore faded jeans that bore the crease of an iron, and a pale blue cotton button-down. The long sleeves seemed ridiculous in this weather, but David had always been a natty dresser. They had all teased him about it when he was a kid.

"Aubrey, come in!" He looked past her at Beau's retreating Mustang. "Who dropped you off?"

"Beau Maddox," she said as she stepped inside.

David's jaw dropped. "How is that possible?"

"A strange set of circumstances, I'll be the first to

admit. But he literally saved my life last night, so I'm trying to give him the benefit of the doubt.''

"Come on, I think we need to sit down and talk about this. How did he save your life?" David led the way into the plush living room. Not a stick of furniture had changed since Aubrey had been a child. Some of the upholstery was new, but the colors hadn't changed—still Chinese red and sapphire blue, with pristine white carpet and white walls. No clutter on the mantle, nothing to mar the symmetry—except a flash of green peeking out from under the sofa.

It looked like a child's toy, Aubrey thought. In fact, it reminded her specifically of Sara's favorite toy, a set of plastic keys on a green ring.

"Aubrey, what's wrong?" David asked as he guided her to the sofa and sat next to her. "What happened last night?"

Aubrey swallowed back the lump trying to form in her throat. "Oh, David, I don't know how to do this except to blurt it out. Patti's dead. The police say she killed herself." She told David everything Lyle had reported this morning, or as much as she could remember. He listened, a stunned expression on his face.

"Are the police sure it was her?" he asked.

"Lyle Palmer knows her, and he identified her. She didn't come here after we talked, did she? She didn't leave Sara here?"

"No. Dear God, are you telling me Sara is missing?"

Aubrey nodded miserably.

David put his face in his hands. "I feel so terrible. When she called, I brushed her off. She said she was in trouble, but she was always saying that, always overdramatizing everything."

"I know. David, don't blame yourself."

"Still, she's my sister. I should have tried harder to get her off drugs and away from those low-life scumbags she hung out with. But you run out of energy and patience, finally. The lies, the little thefts, it wears you down. I guess I gave up on her and now…" He closed his eyes and pressed the bridge of his nose between thumb and forefinger, as if willing back tears. "Shouldn't I have seen the signs?" His voice was thick with emotion. "Shouldn't I have recognized she was suicidal?"

"I don't think she was. I mean, it's crazy, saying she killed herself. I don't mean to speak ill of the dead, but she was too selfish to take that route."

"Are you saying you think someone…murdered her?"

"Yes. This drug dealer she owed money to. He sort of beat me up last night. That's what I meant about Beau saving my life. He was helping me. We were trying to figure out who was threatening Patti, and we found out."

"Aubrey," David said, sounding alarmed, "don't go messing with this stuff. Let the police handle it."

"Beau's an ex-cop."

"He's an idiot if he let you put yourself in danger. No more, I mean it. You're not Batgirl." He paused, seeming to collect himself. "Did you tell the cops you think it was murder?"

"Yes, but Lyle doesn't agree. I'm sure the…autopsy will tell us more." She hated to think about that, hated to even say the word out loud.

"Oh, Aubrey, no. Patti wouldn't want that. Do you have any idea what they do during—"

"We don't have any choice, anyway, David. It's

mandatory with any unexplained death. You're a lawyer, you know that.''

"Damn." He got up suddenly. "Why the hell didn't I listen to her? I could have protected her. She and Sara could have stayed here. Hell, I could have given her the money one more time. What's a few thousand dollars? Certainly not worth killing yourself over.'' He paused. "What about Sara?"

"Lyle thinks Patti must have left Sara someplace safe before she...you know. But then, why didn't she just leave Sara at the baby-sitter's? She made a point of picking her up.''

"Maybe she was going to leave Sara with you. You said she called and asked you to come home, right?''

"Yes, but...I suppose that's possible. Then she got spooked and fled. But if that's the case, where *is* Sara?''

"Are the police even looking for her?''

"Yes, but they aren't treating the matter with any urgency.''

"Damn cops. I'll tell you one thing. When they find her, I'm going to be a better uncle. I'll adopt her! I'll treat her as if she were my own child. I'll give her the stable life she never would have had with Patti.''

Aubrey bristled at the criticism of Patti. She started to object, but then she remembered David hadn't been around Patti in the last year, when she'd turned her life around. Instead she said, "Patti named me as Sara's guardian in her will.''

David looked up, startled. "Really? Well, you aren't stuck with it. It's not binding. The courts have to decide who gets custody, though they'll take her wishes under consideration.''

"Oh. Well, I just thought I'd mention it.''

"Do you want Sara?" he asked bluntly.

"Oh, yes. Yes, I really do."

"I suppose you'd be a good parent," he conceded. "I don't know much about children. But we don't have to worry about that now. First we have to find her."

Neither said anything for a couple of minutes. Finally Aubrey remembered that there was someone else they needed to tell. "David? How's Uncle Wayne? How's he going to take this?"

David shrugged. "He's actually better today. He got up, got dressed. We had breakfast together. I left him reading the paper. Oh, God, it won't be in the paper, will it?"

"No. They think she died yesterday afternoon, but they only found her this morning."

"We better go tell Dad. He's in the breakfast room."

Aubrey was shocked by her uncle's appearance. He'd lost at least thirty pounds since the last time she'd seen him, and his golf shirt and khaki pants hung on his thin frame, giving him a scarecrow appearance. His once-thick silver hair stuck out in wispy clumps on his head. His eyes and cheeks were sunken, and his complexion was a ghastly yellow.

When he looked up and saw Aubrey, however, he smiled and his blue eyes twinkled like David's, and Aubrey recognized the uncle she remembered.

"Aubrey, dear, how lovely to see you. Come give your uncle a hug."

She did. His body felt frail when she clasped him, and he wobbled unsteadily. "Uncle Wayne, why didn't you tell me you'd been ill? I'd have come much sooner. I'm ashamed I stayed away so long."

"I don't blame you, dear," he said, reclaiming his seat. "Sit down, sit down. Would you like some coffee? Beronica can brew us up a fresh pot."

"Beronica?"

"Our new housekeeper," David explained. "She's young, and hardly speaks any English, but she's wonderful."

"I didn't think anyone could replace Esther when she retired, but this Mexican girl is dynamite," Wayne added.

"That's nice, but I don't need any coffee." She looked at David. Was he going to say it, or did he want her to? The silence got to her, and she began. "Uncle Wayne, I'm afraid I came here with some terrible news."

She repeated what she'd told David. Wayne listened, his face hardly showing any emotion at all—until she got to the part about Sara.

"You mean to tell me she's missing?" At Aubrey's nod, he flew into a rage. "Damn Patti. I never should have let her keep that baby. I could have had Sara taken away, you know. With enough money and lawyers, I could have done it. Every judge in Payton owes me a favor. I could have brought the child here, had her raised right, kept her safe. Instead I let that slut daughter of mine expose my granddaughter to all kinds of evil influences—"

"Jeez, Dad, come on," David said, sounding distressed. "You don't have to talk about Patti that way. She just died."

"She was bound to come to a bad end. But did she have to endanger Sara as well?"

"We don't know for sure Sara's in danger," Aubrey said, surprised by her uncle's attitude.

"Of course she's in danger. She's the heir to millions of dollars. She's been kidnapped."

Now Aubrey was truly shocked. Sara, his heir? She could understand Wayne cutting Patti out of his will. God knows what she might have done with millions of dollars. But what about David? She looked at her cousin, silently questioning him.

He shrugged. Obviously this news was no surprise to him. Of course, he had oodles of his own money. Even at his young age, he was a very successful attorney and would no doubt soon be named a partner at the law firm.

"Beronica!" Wayne bellowed.

A young, pretty Hispanic woman appeared at the door to the solarium. "Si, *Señor* Wayne?"

"Bring me the phone and my address book. *El teléfono, y el libro con los nombres?*" he asked in some of the worst-pronounced Spanish Aubrey had ever heard. But with the addition of pantomime, Beronica apparently understood, as she disappeared again.

Wayne turned back to David and Aubrey. "I'm calling the police commissioner himself. Then I'm calling every TV station and newspaper within a hundred miles, and I'm offering a million-dollar reward for Sara's safe return. We'll see if that doesn't get some action!"

Aubrey's head spun. "Are you sure that's a good idea? A big reward will bring out every crackpot in the county."

"If it brings my granddaughter back safely, I don't care." Beronica returned with the phone and the address book. Wayne thumbed through the much-amended pages until he found the number he wanted, and he started dialing. "We'll set up a command center here at the house. Aubrey, you'll be in charge of handling and organizing information as it comes in. Hire some help if you need to. Bring in computers. David, you talk to the bank. Get a million in cash. If I don't have that much in my ready-assets account, sell something.'' He cleared his throat. ''Hello? This is Wayne Clarendon. I want Milo Braither on the line, pronto.''

David took Aubrey's arm and led her out of the breakfast room.

''Do you think this is such a good idea?'' Aubrey asked him once they were safely out of earshot.

David shrugged. ''I don't know. But I haven't seen him this animated in a long time. He suddenly seems like his old self. And, hell, maybe the reward *will* produce results. It's hard to hide a baby. Surely someone has seen or heard Sara, and they'll respond.''

''Maybe,'' Aubrey said, still not sure. But Wayne was going to go ahead with his plans, with or without her help, so she supposed she might as well try to make things go as smoothly as possible.

''What did he mean when he said Sara was his heir?'' Aubrey asked. ''What are you, chopped liver?''

Again, David shrugged. ''He didn't exactly cut me out of the will. He's leaving me the house. And after he dies, I'll probably make partner in the firm.''

A million-dollar house was better than a poke in the eye with a sharp stick, Aubrey supposed. As for being named partner, David had earned that himself. And that left millions and millions of dollars—going to Sara.

''He set up a trust for Sara, I assume,'' she said.

He looked at her as if she were crazy. "Are you telling me you don't know?"

"Know what?"

"Of course there's a trust. And you're the trustee."

Chapter Eight

Aubrey didn't have much time to ponder what David had told her. She suddenly became very busy setting up a press conference and a command center in Wayne's study. By ten o'clock, news of the missing child and the reward was on every TV station, and phone calls began trickling in.

She was grateful for the frantic activity. If she'd stopped for even a moment, she'd have had to think about Beau and the unpleasant way they'd parted. Instead she sat at Wayne's massive desk, the phone glued to her ear, logging phone calls and tips into a computer. Each tip had to be connected with the caller's name, address and phone, in case any of them paid off.

Most of the tips were so vague as to be useless. And then there were the crackpots, who claimed Sara had been kidnapped by aliens, or that they'd had a psychic vision and the baby was "near the big water."

Only one call really stood out, and that one was from Summer—the hostile woman from Greg Holmes's insurance agency. She declined to give her name, but Aubrey recognized her voice.

"I've been close to Patti for the past few months,"

she said, "and I think I know what she did with her baby."

Aubrey held her breath. Summer might have been in a position to know more than anyone. "Yes, please continue."

"I think she sold Sara on the black market. She needed money really bad. And then, overcome with guilt over what she'd done, she killed herself."

Aubrey's hopes plummeted. She'd never heard a more preposterous suggestion. However desperate Patti had been, she loved Sara fiercely.

"How do you know she needed money?" Aubrey asked, trying not to tip Summer off that she'd blown her cover. Perhaps if Summer still thought she was anonymous, she would reveal more.

"She owed money to a drug dealer."

So, she did know more. "Which drug dealer?"

"I dunno. She was paying him off a little at a time, but then he caught her holding out on him. He said if Patti didn't pay off her debt, he was going to make an example out of her."

Aubrey typed in the information as fast as she could. The call was being recorded, so she had a backup, but she wanted to get it down now. This was direct evidence that Cory might be involved in Patti's death.

Summer hung up pretty quickly after that, but Aubrey was energized. She had something concrete she could give the police. She printed out the transcript of the phone call. She was about to call Lyle when the intercom buzzed, and she discovered that Lyle had come to her—and he wasn't happy.

She opened the gates to let him in. When she admitted him through the front door, the detective stood there scowling at her. His tie was loose, and patches of sweat marred his long-sleeved dress shirt.

"Do you have any idea the can of worms you've opened?" he said without preamble.

"I know, Lyle, I know. Come in, please."

She led Lyle into the living room. "Please, sit down."

But he didn't sit. "A million dollars? What were you thinking? People have gone completely nuts. The police station is flooded with calls. Every bounty hunter in the country is no doubt on his way here, hoping to cash in."

She didn't want to think about bounty hunters, or one bounty hunter in particular.

"The reward wasn't my idea," she said firmly. "But think about it. If Patti had given Sara to some innocent person to watch, surely that person would have come forward."

Lyle pursed his lips and turned away from her, looking out the front window. "That's another reason I'm here. I truly thought the baby would have turned up by now. But since she hasn't, we have to consider the possibility of foul play—kidnapping or—" He cut himself off. "Your uncle seems to think his grandchild was the target, not Patti."

"Maybe. But I just got an interesting phone call." She recounted her conversation with Summer. And then she very carefully described her encounter with Cory the previous night, trying to put a spin on it that wouldn't get her into trouble.

"That was you?" Lyle asked, incredulous.

"Oh, so you heard about it."

"The bar owner was livid about the damage to his

property. Who exactly was it who tore down a solid wood door with a medieval axe?''

''He quite possibly saved my life!''

''Don't tell me. Beau Maddox.''

''Lyle, you're missing the point here. Cory was literally beating me up, wanting information about Patti. He threatened to kill me.''

''Then why didn't you go to the police right after it happened?'' He held up his hand to forestall her answer. ''Never mind, I'll tell you. You were poking your nose where it didn't belong. You were interfering in police business. What if this Cory were a viable suspect? You probably scared him so far underground we'll never find him.''

''What do you mean, *if* he were a suspect?'' Now Aubrey was the one who couldn't believe what she was hearing. ''Summer said he threatened to make an example out of Patti. Now she's dead. You don't consider that suspicious?''

''If he killed Patti, why was he so anxious for you to tell him where she was? Your…encounter with him took place *after* she died.''

That took the wind out of Aubrey's sails in a hurry.

''If he'd killed her,'' Lyle continued relentlessly, ''he would have been doing everything in his power to turn suspicion away from himself. He wouldn't have reacted to anything you said or did.''

Unless he'd planned to kill Aubrey. Then he wouldn't have cared where he cast suspicion. ''The guy's a loose cannon. At least check him out!''

''I will, okay? And I'll check out this Summer, too. Sounds like she had a bit of an ax to grind.'' Lyle paused, taking a few deep breaths. Then he glanced through the transcript. "Have you recorded all the calls this way?"

"Yes. And I have a tape backup."

He gave her a look that said he was reevaluating. "Give me everything you have. It's possible the kidnapper would call in, giving a false tip or whatever. His way of returning to the scene of the crime."

Aubrey did as Lyle asked.

"Look, I'm sorry I blew up at you, okay?" he said when she returned with the transcript of calls. "Maybe I'm a little defensive because I should have taken your worries about Patti and Sara more seriously in the beginning."

"Just promise me you'll do everything you can now."

"Of course I will. The whole damn department is on the case now, thanks to your uncle's arm-twisting. Is he here?"

"He is, but he's very ill with cancer. He went to bed a while ago. His hospice nurse gave him pain medication and a sedative, so he's out." His brief burst of energy that morning had burned itself out pretty quickly, and the stress of the situation had hit him hard.

"How about your cousin? David, right?"

"He's at the bank, arranging for the reward money."

"Okay. I'll try them both later." He gave Aubrey a brief, comforting hug and started to leave the room. Then he stopped, his attention snagged by something on the floor. Aubrey followed his gaze and realized he was looking at the same flash of green that had piqued her curiosity earlier. She'd forgotten all about it.

He reached down to pick it up. Aubrey quietly gasped. It was a set of plastic keys on a green ring.

"Patti and Sara never came here, did they?" he asked.

"Not recently." Aubrey kept it to herself that she recognized the toy, but her mind raced. Why would David lie about his sister's visit?

Lyle laid the toy keys on the end table. "Tell David when you see him, I'll definitely be back."

AFTER ANOTHER HOUR of taking phone calls, Aubrey needed a break. She slipped out onto a flagstone terrace through a set of double doors. They used to be delicate French doors with small-paned windows, but now they were solid wood, far more secure.

David had said Uncle Wayne had become increasingly paranoid after the Peeping Tom prowler incident, adding all sorts of security measures—like the keypad at the front gates, and bars on the windows, and double-keyed dead bolts on every door. Given the value of some of the artwork in the Clarendon home, Aubrey supposed it was better safe than sorry.

She left the door open a crack so she could hear the phone, then sat on the low wall that surrounded the patio, her back against the bumpy limestone bricks that made up the house. The air was still and muggy, but it was a switch from the stale, climate-controlled air inside, and it was fresh. She inhaled deeply. The scent of honeysuckle filled her nose. She could hear the faint drone of bees as they visited the flowering vine that climbed up one wall of the house.

She'd forgotten how much she loved this old house, which other than the added security had changed so little over the years. When they were children, she and her brother and cousins had run wild here in the summers like a pack of coyotes, cavorting on the endless expanse of green lawn, playing hide-and-seek in the woods behind the house, or swimming in the huge pool.

In poor weather, the inside of the house had provided a wealth of entertaining features—two floors plus an attic apartment; a back staircase into the kitchen, perfect for games of cops and robbers featuring daring escapes and dramatic shoot-outs. There was even a dumbwaiter, big enough that a child could ride up and down in it, even though they'd been forbidden to do so.

Aubrey smiled at the memory. How innocent those times had been, their childish lives so dull they'd had to invent drama to keep themselves entertained.

Now Aubrey had more drama than she could shake a stick at. And the dumbwaiter, she'd noticed earlier, was being used to store mixing bowls.

She supposed Beronica simply carried trays up the stairs when the need arose.

Something brushed against her arm, startling her. She turned her head and came face to face with Beau, who was semiconcealed in a bush.

"Beau!"

"Shhh!"

"You scared me to death. What are you doing, skulking around in the bushes like a cat burglar?"

"Will you lower your voice? I'm not exactly high on the Clarendons' list of favorite people. If Wayne or David find me here, they're liable to have me arrested."

"Wayne's asleep and David's not here," she said as her heart rate returned to something close to normal.

"As for getting arrested, you better steer clear of the cops anyway. You're in trouble for breaking that door down at Kink."

Beau rolled his eyes. "I was saving your life, in case you'd forgotten."

"I haven't forgotten." She also hadn't forgotten that Beau Maddox was a mercenary jerk she'd been a fool to sleep with. What had she been thinking? His refusal to look for Sara had swept away any romantic illusions she'd been constructing. "I'm just reporting what Lyle told me."

"Listen, Aubrey." He seemed suddenly serious. "I talked to Craig Cartwright—my old partner?"

She nodded.

"Craig's just about the only cop on the force I totally trust, and he told me something interesting. He said Patti's supposed suicide looked fishy to him."

"I told you that already."

"Yeah, but Craig talked to the evidence techs who processed the scene. They said Lyle Palmer's prints were on everything—all over that car."

That wasn't a revelation Aubrey had been expecting. "He was the first detective on the scene, though, right?"

"And he knows better than to touch anything. The uniforms would have ascertained Patti was dead, so there was no need for Palmer to touch anything at all. I'll admit he's a sloppy investigator, but that seems excessive."

"Are you saying you think he's involved in Patti's death?"

"He had no reason to like her. She blew him off pretty thoroughly that time at Dudley's, remember?"

Aubrey did remember. Patti hadn't just ignored his

flirtations. She'd humiliated him in front of his peers, the older cops he'd been trying to impress as a rookie.

"If Lyle was somehow involved in Patti's death," Aubrey said, trying to reason it out, "he had hours and hours to doctor that crime scene before she was found."

"He might not have wanted to risk sticking around and being spotted. And maybe he figured he wouldn't have to. If he made sure he was first on the scene, he could explain away any evidence—fingerprints, hair— that led back to him."

Aubrey shook her head. "That's nuts."

"Maybe so. Best case scenario, though, he's a rotten detective. Which is why you need someone else working this case."

"Like you, perchance?"

He smiled. "Yeah. You were right all along. Sara's been missing too long now. I'm going to find her for you."

Beau looked at her as if he expected her to throw her arms around him in gratitude. Instead she folded her arms.

"That's very noble of you, Beau. And I suppose the one-million-dollar reward had nothing to do with your change of heart."

His jaw dropped. "The *what?*"

"Oh, like you don't know anything about it. Are you going to stand there and pretend you suddenly developed a conscience?"

"Aubrey, I don't know anything about any reward."

"And I suppose you've been living under a rock for the past few hours?"

''Would you just tell me what you're talking about?''

She opened her mouth to tell him off when a chunk of limestone from directly over her head exploded outward, just as a popping noise sounded from the woods on the other side of the wrought-iron fence.

Aubrey didn't fully comprehend what was going on until Beau yelled ''Down!'' He leaped over the wall, taking her with him, and threw her onto the patio, though he came along with her, twisting at the last minute to take the brunt of the fall onto his body.

Someone was shooting at them.

Beau's hard body pressed her down into the sharp flagstones. She heard a louder reverberation and realized Beau was shooting back. Good heavens, where had his gun come from? They'd spent the previous day together and she'd never noticed him carrying a gun, but apparently he was.

The double doors opened, and Aubrey recognized the string of rapid Spanish as belonging to Beronica. Then Beronica screamed.

Beau rolled sideways, releasing Aubrey. ''Get inside. Crawl, don't stand up. Call the cops, and stay away from the windows.''

''Where are you going?''

Before she could ask again, he was gone. Oh, heavens, he was going to look for trouble. Why couldn't he just come inside with her and wait for the cops? But no, he had to play hero.

Aubrey got to her hands and knees and crawled, as directed, to the patio door. Beronica helped her inside, still spewing Spanish.

''Beronica, *por favor, en el Inglés,*'' Aubrey said,

drawing on her pitiful skills in Spanish. *"Yo no comprendo el Español."*

"Who that man?" Beronica asked.

Aubrey answered as she went to the kitchen to dial 911. "He's a friend. *Amigo.* A private investigator, sort of. He wants to help find Sara." She could see that Beronica didn't quite understand. "An investigator—like Magnum, P.I.?"

At that Beronica nodded. *"Sí,* Magnum. He shoots the gun?"

"Yes, but someone else is shooting the gun, too."

BEAU SCALED the iron fence close to the house, then worked his way from tree to tree back to the area from which he thought the shots had come. All the while, his mind teemed with more questions than answers.

The bullet could have been intended for either him or Aubrey—it had whizzed past his ear on the way to the wall just inches above Aubrey's head. But no one had known he was on the property, so he had to conclude Aubrey was the likely target.

Who would want to kill Aubrey, and why? Cory the bartender came to mind first. After Beau's visit earlier, Craig had gone to check up on Cory Silvan at his last known address. He wasn't there, and it appeared he'd packed up and left in a hurry. Something had sure spooked him. Maybe he thought Aubrey would sic the cops on him for what he did last night. Or maybe he was on the defensive for some other reason—like murder and kidnapping.

If he thought Aubrey knew more than she did, he might want to eliminate her. But how would Cory have known she was here? Beau wished he knew more about this reward. Had Aubrey been on TV? That

The Harlequin Reader Service® — Here's how it works:

NO POSTAGE
NECESSARY
IF MAILED
IN THE
UNITED STATES

BUSINESS REPLY MAIL
FIRST-CLASS MAIL   PERMIT NO. 717-003   BUFFALO, NY

POSTAGE WILL BE PAID BY ADDRESSEE

HARLEQUIN READER SERVICE
3010 WALDEN AVE
PO BOX 1867
BUFFALO NY 14240-9952

If offer card is missing write to: The Harlequin Reader Service, 3010 Walden Ave., P.O. Box 1867, Buffalo, NY 14240-1867

Do You Have the LUCKY KEY?

PLAY THE Lucky Key Game

and you can get

FREE BOOKS and a FREE GIFT!

Scratch the gold areas with a coin. Then check below to see the books and gift you can get!

YES!

I have scratched off the gold areas. Please send me the 2 FREE BOOKS and GIFT for which I qualify. I understand I am under no obligation to purchase any books, as explained on the back of this card.

(H-I-02/04)

© 2002 HARLEQUIN ENTERPRISES LTD. ® and ™ are trademarks owned by Harlequin Enterprises Ltd.

382 HDL DVGA   182 HDL DVGQ

FIRST NAME   LAST NAME

ADDRESS

APT.#   CITY

STATE/PROV.   ZIP/POSTAL CODE

🔑🔑🔑🔑 2 free books plus a free gift   🔑🔑🔑 1 free book

🔑🔑🔑🔑 2 free books   🔑🔑🔑 Try Again!

Offer limited to one per household and not valid to current Harlequin Intrigue® subscribers. All orders subject to approval. Credit or Debit balances in a customer's account(s) may be offset by any other outstanding balance owed by or to the customer.

Visit us online at www.eHarlequin.com

could bring out any number of crazies, Cory among them.

Beau found the spot where the shooter had hidden himself, behind a massive live oak tree. He was probably long gone, but the guy had gotten careless and left a couple of 9-millimeter shell casings on the ground.

Last night's rain had left the ground soft enough to reveal one partial footprint. Stepping on leaves and stones and bark to avoid leaving prints of his own, Beau examined the print. It was pretty indistinct, probably not good enough to make a definitive match. All Beau could tell was that it had been made by a man-sized athletic shoe.

He decided to collect the shell casings. If he left it to Lyle, the clod would probably get his own prints all over them, like he'd done with Patti's car, rendering the evidence useless. Beau would have to see if he could find the bullet on the patio, too. He used a twig to retrieve the two casings so as not to damage any evidence. He had nothing to put them in, however, so he placed them gently in the breast pocket of his black T-shirt.

The bullet from Beau's gun was lodged in the live oak tree. He was gratified to see that his aim had been accurate, though he wished he'd hit the bastard. As a purely self-protective gesture, he used his pocketknife to dig the bullet out of the tree. He tucked the bullet into his jeans pocket for later disposal, then disguised the hole in the bark with a bit of mud. If the Payton Police Department evidence techs did their usual lousy job, the hole would never be found.

By the time he returned to the house, the cops had arrived, lights flashing. Lyle among them, unfortunately. Aubrey had just opened the door to let Lyle and two uniforms into the house. Beau caught up to them and entered last, earning a scowl from Aubrey.

"Well, well, look who we have here," Lyle said smugly when he realized Beau had joined them. "Hope you have a real good reason for creeping around on this estate."

"Oh, for heaven's sake," Aubrey said, exasperated. "He was standing right next to me when the shots were fired."

"Shots?" Lyle said. "More than one?"

Aubrey's gaze flickered toward Beau, then back to Lyle. "I'm not sure. I thought I heard two, but maybe one was an echo." She guided them through the house to the heavy wooden doors that led to the patio. "I was right out here. The shots came from that area, I think." She pointed in the general direction of the live oak tree, which was two hundred feet away. "And one bullet hit here on the wall, just above my head."

Lyle inspected the damage to the limestone wall. The bullet, Beau could now see, was lodged in the rock. To his horror, Lyle climbed on the retaining wall and started to dig the bullet out with his own pocketknife.

Beau exchanged a look with one of the uniforms, a young African-American woman whose name tag identified her as Brooks. They shared an understanding—Lyle's actions weren't standard police procedure.

"You might want to leave that there," Beau said, unable to keep quiet. "It hasn't been photographed or measured yet."

Lyle turned toward Beau, his face growing red, the knife held out in an almost threatening gesture. "You stay out of this," he said, "or I'll have you arrested for interfering with a police investigation." Just the same, he stopped digging. "Brooks, go check out that area behind the fence near that big tree. See if you can find any evidence of the shooter."

"Yes, sir."

Beau took the opportunity to follow Brooks as she headed back through the house. "I've already checked it out," he said, hoping Brooks had a less dim view of ex-cops than Palmer. "I'll show you the spot. I collected some shell casings."

"Man, you really are trying to get yourself in trouble." But her gaze held grudging respect. "I've heard of you. You're the one who brought in Gavin Schuyler."

God, he wished he could be famous for something else. Tracking down the Broski heiress had been a helluva lot harder than finding Gavin. But because of a confidentiality agreement he'd had with the heiress's father, no one knew anything about it.

"Just don't mention that in front of Aubrey. She's his sister." He showed Brooks the spot behind the live oak, showed her the footprint and where he'd found the casings, which she bagged up. She also spotted a single strand of hair clinging to a nearby bush.

"It's not mine," Beau said quickly. The hair appeared to be a brownish-blond, nowhere near Beau's dark brown.

"I'm gonna get an evidence tech up here," Brooks said. "I don't want to mess anything up."

Beau nodded his approval. Apparently Payton did have some decent cops in the ranks.

As they returned to the house, a motorcycle roared up the driveway. The gates had been left open, Beau noted, wishing he'd reminded Aubrey to close them behind the cops.

"Who the hell is that?" Brooks asked, quickening her step. Beau was right behind her. They made it to the front door just as the chopper's grungy rider climbed off his bike and made his unsteady way toward them.

The stranger was tall and rangy, wearing ratty cutoff jeans, no shirt, and motorcycle boots similar to the ones Beau often wore. He had dirty-blond hair, two days' growth of beard and enough body art to have kept a tattoo parlor busy for a week.

"Can we help you?" Brooks said, moving to block the door.

"I'm Charlie Soffit," the man said with a belligerent tilt to his head. His words were slightly slurred. He was obviously under the influence of something. He waited, as if his name explained everything. When Brooks made no reply, he continued impatiently. "I'm Patti's—I'm Sara's father, damn it. I want to know why I wasn't notified my baby's missing—oh, God, I'm gonna kill that bitch Aubrey!"

Chapter Nine

As Aubrey, Lyle and the other cop left the patio and returned inside, they all heard raised voices that sounded as if they were coming from the front porch. Lyle and the uniform rushed toward the noise, Aubrey right behind. When they opened the door, a strange sight greeted them. The female cop and Beau were on the ground in the driveway, grappling with a stranger.

"Thanks for the quick action, boys," the woman cop said, one plucked eyebrow arched in sarcasm. "But with Maddox's help here, things are under control. This might be our shooter."

As soon as the cop and Beau hauled the man to his feet, Aubrey realized he wasn't a stranger after all. "Charlie, what are you doing here?"

"You could have called me," he said as he ceased struggling and started sobbing. "I loved her, and you didn't even tell me she was dead. I had to hear it on the TV! And now my kid's missing."

Lyle looked at Aubrey. "Who is this guy?"

"Charlie Soffit. Patti lived with him for a while. He is, unfortunately, Sara's father." She turned her attention back to Charlie. "You don't have any rights where Patti or Sara are concerned. You kicked her out

after you got her pregnant. And you signed that paper—''

"I did not kick her out!,'' he interrupted. "She left
me. I wanted to marry her. I wanted to do right by
her. But she wouldn't let me get near that baby. My
own flesh and blood.''

"This isn't getting us anywhere,'' Lyle said in disgust. "Brooks, why do you think he's the shooter?''

"The first words out of his mouth were that he
wanted to kill Aubrey,'' Brooks said.

A chill wiggled up Aubrey's spine. She knew she
wasn't Charlie's favorite person. He'd always claimed
Aubrey had turned Patti against him, that Aubrey was
the reason they broke up.

"What shooter?'' Charlie asked. "What are you
talking about? I didn't shoot nobody.''

"Check his bike,'' Lyle told the other cop. "See if
he's got a gun.''

"Don't we need a warrant?'' the cop said.

"We've got probable cause. Do it.''

Reluctantly, the cop opened first one of the huge
motorcycle's saddlebags, then the other. He reached
in and withdrew a large handgun. "This what we're
looking for?''

Aubrey felt light-headed at the sight of the gun. She
only hoped Lyle's haste wouldn't make the evidence
inadmissible.

"Let's take him in,'' Lyle said.

"Just a minute,'' Beau said. He still stood close to
Charlie, though he was no longer holding him.
"What's this gash on your arm, dude?''

Aubrey hadn't noticed it before. But Charlie did indeed have a ragged cut on his right forearm.

"A dog bit me. Why?''

"A dog? Are you sure?" Beau asked. "Not a person?"

"Yeah, a pit bull. They don't like motorcycles."

Aubrey waited for Lyle to respond. But he just stood there, apparently not understanding the significance. Maybe he really was a lousy cop. He sure had a short memory.

Beau shook his head. "Have someone photograph that wound. And swab his hands, for God's sake."

Lyle looked supremely irritated. "Maddox, will you just stay out of it?"

"Someone's got to do your job for you."

"Look, turkey. I could haul your ass in for—"

"Enough!" Aubrey interrupted, stepping between the two men before they could come to blows. "Don't you dare put him in jail," she said to Lyle. "Whether you like him or not, he's good at finding people. Let him help."

Lyle narrowed his gaze at Beau. "Just stay the hell out of my way."

Beau looked as though he was biting his tongue to keep from retorting.

"And you," Lyle said, pointing his finger at Aubrey. "Lock that gate after us, and don't let anyone in for any reason." He softened his voice. "And keep recording the calls you get. Maybe one of those tips will pay off."

AUBREY CHECKED the answering machine. A couple of calls had come in during all the excitement, but they didn't seem significant. She dutifully recorded them on the computer, then she let Beau scroll through all the other tips.

He stopped at the one from Summer. "Interesting.

She seems to confirm that Cory's the one we need to look at."

"What about Charlie?" Aubrey asked. "Patti did refuse to let him have any contact with Sara—he was telling the truth about that. He apparently regretted severing his parental rights. He tried to get back together with her and she wouldn't have anything to do with him. Not that I blame her."

"He does make a handy suspect," Beau said. "Unfortunately, I don't think he's the shooter. He was wearing motorcycle boots. The footprint I saw up in the woods was definitely from an athletic shoe. Also, I think Charlie was too drunk or doped up to shoot as accurately as our guy did."

"He could have changed shoes. He could have been a lucky shot."

"Possible."

"What about the bite mark on his arm?" she asked, unwilling to dismiss Charlie. "He could have come to my house looking for Patti and Sara, and he got me instead."

"Definitely possible," Beau said. "We might also be dealing with two different perps. Or maybe a gang. Either Charlie or Cory could have hired a shooter once they found out about the reward."

"Two different people trying to kill me?" Aubrey scoffed. "I'm a chemistry professor, for God's sake."

"Yesterday you were just in the wrong place. Today you were definitely the target."

She sighed. "There's one other thing I should show you." She led him into the living room where she'd left the set of plastic keys. She handed them to Beau. "I'm ashamed to even bring this up. But it's so peculiar. David said in no uncertain terms that he has not seen Patti in months. But this is Sara's favorite toy—or one just like it. I found it under the sofa.''

Beau examined the keys, then shook them, causing a tinkling sound. ''It's a pretty common toy.''

''But what's it doing here?''

''Does Beronica have any children?''

Aubrey shrugged. ''I don't know. Let's ask her.''

When they went to the kitchen, they found Beronica busily preparing lunch, though it was almost midafternoon.

''Sorry I so late,'' she said as she pulled a pan of steaming enchiladas out of the oven. ''Everything so crazy today.''

Aubrey hadn't felt like eating since she'd heard about Patti, but she knew she should eat something. The Mexican food made her stomach growl. ''Beau, would you like some?'' she asked politely.

''Sure.''

Aubrey got out two plates and heaped them with enchiladas, beans, and rice, while Beronica prepared trays for Wayne and Mary, the hospice nurse.

''Beronica, do you have any small children?'' Aubrey asked. *''Niños? Bebés?''* She pantomimed rocking a baby.

Beronica smiled. ''Oh, *sí.* I have a little boy, Carlos. He one year old.''

''And does he live here with you?''

She nodded. ''But during the day, my sister take care of him. He make cry, you know, and I no want him to wake Señor Wayne.''

Aubrey was much relieved to find a logical explanation for the toy. Beau gave her a look that said *I told you so.*

When Beronica finished the trays, she skillfully balanced them both in her arms and headed out of the kitchen.

"Why doesn't she use the dumbwaiter for that?" Beau asked. "It goes right up to the master bedroom, doesn't it?"

"I don't think anyone uses it." Aubrey got up and went to the sliding wooden door in the kitchen wall and opened it, revealing the heavy ceramic mixing bowls stacked inside. "Maybe it doesn't work anymore." She hadn't recalled the dumbwaiter being so small. "Is it really possible I used to ride in this thing?" She gave a delicate shiver, recalling the thrill of getting closed into the claustrophobic space and moving through the dark shaft.

"You and David were always inventing crazy scenarios that involved smuggling children in and out of various places."

Aubrey smiled at the memories. She and Patti—and even David—had used the dumbwaiter to escape all manner of imaginary Nazis, cruel orphanages, and Soviet spies.

"We had so much fun back then," she said wistfully. "What happened to us?"

"We grew up," Beau said simply. "Pretend cops and robbers became real."

And hormones kicked in, Aubrey added silently. Her unrequited crush on Beau had transformed the carefree games of little girls and boys to miserable ordeals of rising hopes and crashing disappointments. Also, Beau's and Gavin's brushes with the law had pitted them against her parents, as well as Uncle Wayne and Aunt Joan. The freedom Aubrey had taken for granted—to ride around with the boys, hang out at

Stubby's, or just roam the neighborhood at night—had been severely restricted.

Then Aunt Joan's death when Aubrey was seventeen had put an end to childhood.

Beau checked his watch. "I've got to get to work. Some of those tips are worth checking out. Long shots, but the kind of things cops will overlook because they don't have the time or manpower. If you learn anything that might be helpful, call the First Strike office. Lori will get hold of me."

"I want to go with you," she said suddenly. The idea of just sitting here, answering the phone, was unappealing. Calls were still coming in, and there would be peaks of activity every time the reward was publicized. But the task had become boring. "You might need me. You said yourself, I'm pretty good at getting people to talk."

"Like Cory? No, I'm not making that mistake again." He took one last bite of enchilada. "You stay here. Wayne has turned this house into a fortress. You're safe, as long as you stay behind locked doors, and that's where I want you."

She folded her arms. "I hate it when you order me around."

"Tough. If you want me to help, you play by my rules."

"Like you'd quit looking for Sara? With that million-dollar reward out there?"

He huffed out an exasperated sigh. "It's not about the damn money. Hell, if I earn the reward, I'll give it back. I'll donate it to charity."

"Oh, that I'd like to see. The Charity for Underprivileged Bounty Hunters?"

"You really don't have a clue what drives me, do you?"

"I know all I need to know."

Beau laid down his fork and went to the paper-towel dispenser. He ripped off a sheet and wiped his mouth. Aubrey realized she'd forgotten to get them napkins.

"When will you be back?" she asked, hating the needy quality in her voice. It was just that she felt safer when he was around.

"You sound as if you might actually miss me."

"Don't hold your breath."

"I hope I won't have to come back until I have Sara." He turned and walked out of the kitchen.

Aubrey took their plates to the sink. She'd hardly touched her food. She wished she could make herself stop quarreling with Beau. But every time they were getting along, she felt her physical attraction to him rearing its ugly head, found herself wanting to be close to him. She knew those feelings would get her into trouble. So she deliberately picked a fight, reminding herself in the process that she could not trust her heart where Beau Maddox was concerned. She had to trust her brain.

BEAU CHECKED out as many leads as he could during the next couple of hours. Most of them were completely bogus, though his visit to Greg Holmes's office produced more questions than answers.

The outer door was locked, though it was only three-thirty in the afternoon. But there was a bell. He rang it several times, hoping to rouse Greg, if he was working in his inner sanctum.

Through the window, Beau could just make out the office interior. He was about to give up when he saw the inner door open. But it wasn't Greg who appeared—it was Summer. And she was adjusting her clothing in a telltale way.

He suddenly recalled Summer's comment about Patti from yesterday—"She's banging her boss." Looked like Patti wasn't the only one.

Summer jerked the door open. "What do you want?"

"Any reason you're so hostile toward me?"

"It's just that I'm busy, and I told y'all everything I knew yesterday."

"Except that part about Patti owing money to a drug dealer, and how he'd threatened to make an example of her? That's what you told the tip line, right?"

Summer's eyes widened to the size of quarters. "How did you know that?"

"Your voice is distinctive. So how come you didn't tell us that last night?"

Summer inched toward the door, but Beau kept himself between her and any possible escape. "It slipped my mind. I didn't think of it until I heard on the news that she'd offed herself. And I started thinking about it. I wouldn't put it past Patti to do something like sell her own baby. I thought the cops should think about all possibilities, you know?"

"Or maybe you wanted to throw them off, in case they started to suspect what really happened to Patti."

Summer's nostrils flared. "You're not, like, accusing me of anything, are you?"

"Just thinking about all possibilities, like you said. A woman is perfectly capable of killing a romantic rival."

Summer's mouth moved, but no sound came out.

"I'm not saying that's what happened," Beau said.

If the police were right about Patti's time of death, it would have occurred during work hours. Summer would have had a hard time getting away from the office for long enough to cook up a fake suicide scene, kill Aubrey, and hide the baby. But he wouldn't rule out the possibility. "But it might occur to the police. The fact you gave them a bogus lead might not reflect too favorably on you."

"I didn't call the police," Summer said. "I called that tip line, the one Patti's father set up."

Beau shrugged. "Your call has already been turned over to the cops. Along with your identity. I'm surprised they haven't been here." But he wasn't really surprised, as incompetent as Lyle Palmer was.

Summer cast a worried look over her shoulder at the door she'd just emerged from. Then she lowered her voice. "Look, it wasn't my idea to call. Greg told me to do it. This office isn't exactly on the up-and-up. He's the one who doesn't want the police snooping around here."

Now here was an interesting twist. "What do you mean by, 'not on the up-and-up'?"

"He writes policies on people who don't really qualify for life insurance. Then he takes kickbacks when they die. And I never told you any of this," she said hurriedly as the door opened and Greg emerged.

He scowled at Beau. "What now?"

"Just checking up on a few details." He debated about whether to put Summer on the spot and reveal to Greg what she'd just told him. Then he decided she might be a good source for him later if he protected her now. He wanted to know more about the phony insurance scam. If Patti knew about it, if she was romantically entangled with Holmes, it's possible she'd threatened to blow the whistle on him if he didn't leave his wife or pay her money. Certainly *that* would be a strong motive for murder.

"Look," Holmes said, grabbing Beau by the upper arm. "I'm happy to answer questions for the cops. But I don't see you flashing a badge, so I don't owe you any explanations. I want you out of this office, and I don't want to see you again."

Beau resisted the urge to flatten Greg Holmes with one well-placed punch to the nose. Getting slapped with an assault charge wouldn't help him find Sara. So he let Holmes manhandle him out the door as Summer looked on wearing a smug smile.

Still, Beau didn't let Holmes have the last word. "I have friends on the Payton police force. One word from me, and they'd be all over you like ducks on a june bug. So I might tone down the hostility if I were you."

Holmes's mouth went slack as he considered the implications. Beau left him with a smile.

The smile didn't last long, though. He still didn't have any strong leads that would help him find Sara. And the longer she was missing, the shorter the chances of finding her unharmed—especially because there had been no ransom demand.

He was hungry, he realized. He wished he'd eaten more of those first-rate enchiladas at the Clarendon house. But it had been hard to enjoy his meal with Aubrey sitting across the table from him, accusing him of being a coldhearted, mercenary bastard.

He wished there was some way to get past her barriers. It amazed him that she'd let him be intimate with her physically while she so totally mistrusted his motives. Maybe it would help when, a couple of months from now, he testified at Gavin's parole hearing. He'd put Gavin in prison, but maybe helping him get out would make Aubrey—

He cursed viciously. Why was he worried about this? Why did Aubrey's forgiveness matter? She was a pipe dream, a teenage fantasy he was determined to hold on to. He and Aubrey had nothing in common except the past...and one unforgettable sexual encounter.

One big, incredible mistake.

He headed for Dudley's Blue Note, where he'd arranged to meet Craig. Craig had heard a few things through the grapevine and wanted to fill Beau in. Unlike Lyle Palmer, Craig had always welcomed Beau's help on a case. But Craig wasn't big on taking credit or receiving commendations or congratulatory phone calls from the mayor. He just wanted to get the job done, whatever it took.

Sara Clarendon wasn't Craig's case, but that didn't stop him from wanting to see it cleared.

Dudley's was quiet tonight, Beau thought as he claimed a stool at the bar and ordered himself a Bud. One booth was filled with uniforms, rookies Beau didn't know. With each passing day, he felt more and more out of touch with the department.

Craig swung through the revolving door a few minutes later. He'd changed out of his work clothes and into ragged running shorts and a T-shirt, and he carried a gym bag. He spotted Beau, nodded toward the back, then headed that way. Apparently he didn't want to sit where a lot of people would see them together.

"I'd be skewered if anyone knew I was doing this," Craig said without preamble. "But I copied the case file as well as Patti's rap sheet for you. I can't give it to you in here, but we can walk out together. It's in the gym bag.''

"Why the cloak and dagger?"

"Palmer's on my case. He's in charge of the Clarendon baby kidnapping, and he doesn't want anyone upstaging him."

"Are they actually calling it a kidnapping now?"

"Palmer is. Anything to puff up his image."

"How about the shell casings?"

"The ident section found one clear fingerprint."

"Yes!" Beau was elated at the news. If they could identify the shooter, they might find Sara. Though Beau hadn't figured out how it all fit together, he was reasonably sure it did.

"Don't get too excited," Craig said. "They put it in AFIS, but so far they haven't found a match."

AFIS was the Automated Fingerprint Identification System. Every felon and every person arrested in the whole country had had his fingerprints entered into the system, as had other people fingerprinted for legitimate security reasons—like cops.

"Hell." That meant it was likely the shooter didn't have a police record. That most likely eliminated Charlie and Cory. And Lyle Palmer. Beau was ashamed to admit he was hoping Lyle had gotten himself involved in a murder, or at least a coverup. He hadn't forgotten the detective's unprofessional behavior at the scene of Patti's death, and more recently he told Craig about the iffy search of Lyle's motorcycle, and Lyle trying to dig the bullet out of the wall with his knife.

"The guy is a menace," Craig agreed. "But more stupid than evil, I think."

"I have a couple more suspects for you." Beau told Craig about Greg Holmes and Summer. Craig didn't take notes, but he didn't have to. He had almost perfect recall of any conversation. "And I have one more idea—just a vague suspicion, really. It's Patti's brother, David."

"Oh, we're checking out both him and Wayne, don't worry." Every cop knew that violent crimes were committed more often between family members than strangers.

"I did a little illegal search earlier today," Beau said. "I climbed the fence at the Clarendon estate and sneaked into the house. David has a home office there."

Craig groaned. "Maddox, you're a disgrace. I can't use anything you found."

Beau took a sip of his beer and said nothing.

"So, what did you find? You could at least steer me in the right direction."

"David Clarendon is into some serious, serious debt."

"Oh, that. Yeah, we already found that out. A huge mortgage on his own house, and a vacation house in Sedona. A Porsche. At least seven credit cards, all of them maxed out. But the guy's pulling in a healthy six figures. Most people earning that much money do rack up some debts. And we didn't see any evidence it's about to crash in on him."

Beau felt a sense of relief to hear Craig dismiss David's debt as a motive for murder. David had never been Beau's favorite person in the world, but he was Aubrey's cousin.

"You have a history with this guy, right?"

"Known him since he was a snot-nosed kid. He was

quite the manipulator. All the adults loved him, all the other kids hated him.'' Except Aubrey. She always gave David the benefit of the doubt, and David had carefully cultivated her loyalty. That was why Beau had to be very careful about expressing any suspicions toward David around her. If he somehow got David in trouble—even if he was guilty—that would be the nail in the coffin of his relationship with Aubrey. Earlier today she'd jumped at the chance to exonerate David of lying.

"Any word on the autopsy?'' Beau asked, changing the subject.

"It's scheduled for tomorrow morning.''

"What about Charlie Soffit? Did they swab his hands?''

Craig shrugged. "I'm out of the loop on that. But Gary over in ballistics already eliminated Soffit's gun as the one that fired the bullet at you and Aubrey.''

"He might have had another gun. He might have disposed of it.'' But Beau realized that, like Aubrey, he was grasping at straws. Soffit probably wasn't the shooter.

"So what are you going to do next?'' Craig asked.

Beau didn't know. He was flat out of leads. His vision of returning to the Clarendon house by night-fall—the triumphant hero with Sara in his arms—was quickly disintegrating.

Chapter Ten

A flurry of tips came after the six-o'clock news, and again at ten. By now Aubrey was so tired she was responding by rote, typing in exactly what everyone said. But she no longer felt able to evaluate the information. The best she could do was fax copies of the transcripts to the police. If they wanted to do something with it, they could. She had to get some rest.

But first, she wanted to talk to her uncle Wayne before he went to sleep. Dinner had been an odd affair, with sporadic, disjointed conversation. Aubrey had sensed a definite tension in the air between David and Wayne, though nothing overt was said. Now she wanted a private word with her uncle.

She found Wayne sitting up in bed, watching TV. He looked even frailer in his pajamas than he had in street clothes. But he managed a strained smile for Aubrey.

"Come in, dear. If I haven't said it before, thank you for all your hard work. You've stuck your neck out for this branch of the family far more than you're obligated to."

"I'm part of this family," she said, pulling up a chair. "I'm so sorry I stayed away for so long. I always thought there would be time later to mend fences."

"Time is the one thing my money can't buy."

"Are you in a lot of pain?" she asked, hoping she wasn't getting too personal.

He shrugged. "Some days are worse than others. It's a worse pain, though, to see your own children die. I never thought I'd have to live through that."

Aubrey hadn't seen Wayne grieve at all for Patti. His concern had seemed to be solely for Sara, until this moment. She realized he had tears in his eyes.

"I still loved her. Even after everything she did— all the lies, the stealing, the drugs, the criminal record. She was an embarrassment to this family, but I still loved her. Maybe if she'd known that, she'd have…" He shrugged.

"But she did turn her life around," Aubrey pointed out. "She was trying, anyway. You have to believe that, Uncle Wayne. She was trying to be a responsible mother, and she loved Sara."

"She did go to the trouble of making out a will," he said thoughtfully. "That surprised me. So out of character for a girl who always indulged in the moment to plan ahead."

"Speaking of wills…I was a bit surprised to learn that you'd left everything to Sara." She tried to sound casual. "And David tells me you named me as trustee."

Wayne nodded. "I don't know why it would surprise you. I certainly couldn't leave that job to Patti."

"But what about David?"

"Oh, he doesn't know anything about raising children. You're close to Sara. You'll do what's best."

"But David…" She didn't know how to put it into words without being rude and nosy.

"Why did I disinherit him?"

"David told me the terms of the will. But he acted like he didn't care."

"Well, he always did have a strange attitude about money," Wayne said dismissively. "It's never been something that worried him, anyway." He paused, picked at some invisible lint on his blanket. "I suppose you think my decision is very arbitrary. But if I'd favored one of my children over the other, the will would surely have been contested in court. No, this way all the money will be evenly divided among my grandchildren. If David has children some day, they'll get a share."

Aubrey supposed her uncle's explanation made some sense. She changed the conversation to more practical matters. "Detective Palmer is sending over an officer to monitor the tip hotline so we can all get some sleep. I didn't want you to be alarmed if you saw a stranger."

"I'll sleep like the dead tonight, dear, don't worry." He shook a pill bottle that had been sitting on his nightstand. "These little wonders will see to that."

Aubrey kissed him on his papery cheek, squeezed his hand and left him to his rest. Poor man.

She said good-night to David, who had agreed to deal with the expected visitor. "No offense, cousin, but you look a mess," he'd told her, giving her an affectionate hug.

She didn't deny it. She'd brought only a minimum of clothing and cosmetics with her when she'd left her house yesterday, a lifetime ago. She hadn't imagined she'd be away for long. Tomorrow she would have to get some more clothes or do laundry.

Beronica had made up a room for Aubrey on the second floor, next door to Wayne's. After taking a warm shower to help her relax, Aubrey climbed into her nightshirt and slid under the covers, grateful for the energetic air-conditioning that kept the hot humidity at bay. Her mind whirled in circles as she closed her eyes, but fatigue won out and she slept.

Sometime in the night she woke from a frightening nightmare. In it she was reaching for Sara, but then someone dropped her down a dark hole. She woke up in a sweat, gasping for breath, the baby's cries still ringing in her ears.

It had sounded so real, she thought as her breathing came harder and harder. Then she realized something was wrong. She couldn't breathe. The telltale, rotten-egg odor of Mercaptan was strong in the air.

Mercaptan was the chemical the gas company added to methane to give it a nasty smell. Oh, God. She jumped out of bed, reached instinctively for the light switch, then stopped herself. She couldn't afford to turn on lights. Any small spark could ignite the methane and cause a lethal explosion.

She opened the door onto the hallway—she had to get everyone out of the house. The air seemed fresher in the hall, or perhaps she was just getting used to the smell.

Wayne's room was closest. She knocked loudly and entered, finding her uncle in a sound sleep. Thankfully a nightlight allowed her to see.

"Uncle Wayne, wake up!" she shouted. "We have to get out of the house!"

He roused slightly, but he was extremely groggy. "What? What's going on?"

David appeared in the doorway, wearing only a pair of sweatpants. "Dad? Aubrey, is he all right?"

"There's a gas leak. Can't you smell it? Help me get your father out."

David reached for the light switch just as she'd done. "No! No lights."

"Right." He rushed over and helped her get Wayne out of bed. Between them they half dragged, half carried him out the door and down the wide, curved staircase.

"Who else is in the house? Beronica?"

"Yes, on the third floor. I'll get her."

"I've got Uncle Wayne. You go. Beronica should be okay. The mix of methane and propane they use in Payton is heavier than nitrogen or oxygen, so it sinks."

Wayne was walking now, though he leaned heavily on Aubrey. "A gas leak?"

She saw him to the entry hall and used the key hanging on a hook by the front door to unlock the dead bolt. "Get as far away from the house as you can," she said. "It might explode."

"Where are you going?"

"To make sure there's no one else here." She ran through all the rooms downstairs, calling out. In the study manning the phone she was surprised to find not the uniformed officer Lyle had promised, but Lyle himself. Wearing jeans and a T-shirt, he was slumped over the desk, asleep.

She hoped.

She shook him. "Lyle, wake up."

He roused slowly. "What?"

"Gas leak. We have to get out of the house."

"Gas leak?" he repeated stupidly.

"Please, Lyle." She tugged on his arm to get him to move. Finally he seemed to understand, and the two of them made it out the front door, though they were both staggering with dizziness.

Aubrey breathed in great gulps of the humid night air until her head cleared. Lyle appeared to be doing the same. Then she looked for her uncle and the others. All she could see was a white lump on the grass, far from the house.

"Oh, my God." She ran toward her uncle's crumpled form. Lyle was right behind her, cell phone in hand. He was already summoning help.

Wayne was conscious, but struggling for breath. "Call for an ambulance," she said.

"No, no ambulance," Wayne managed to say. "I'm in hospice, remember? I'm DNR."

Aubrey looked at Lyle, hoping he might know what that meant.

"Do Not Resuscitate," he said. "It means no heroic lifesaving measures."

"But it's not the cancer that's making him sick," Aubrey said desperately. "It's methane gas."

"I'm all right now anyway," Wayne insisted, sitting up.

Beronica and her baby boy soon joined them. The baby—Carlos, Aubrey remembered—was crying. Was that the baby she'd heard earlier in her dreams? Had he awakened her?

She gave Beronica and Carlos an impulsive hug. "I think you saved our lives, kiddo," she said to the baby, who wasn't listening. "Where's David?"

Beronica's eyes were huge. "He say he go turn off bad air."

"He should leave it for the gas company," Lyle said. "They're on their way. So is the fire department."

Aubrey considered going to look for David. What if he'd gone back inside and passed out? But then she saw him coming around the corner of the house. And he wasn't alone. Was that—could it possibly be…

It was. What was Beau doing here? Aubrey ran to meet them, then skidded to a stop with an involuntary shriek of shock. David had Beau by the arm, and he was aiming a gun at Beau's back.

"Look who I found skulking around in the bushes," David said, a note of triumph in his voice.

"David! Put that thing away. Are you insane?"

"Not until I'm sure he didn't have something to do with that gas leak. Maybe he got inside, blew out all the pilot lights."

Aubrey rolled her eyes. "Even if he did, it would take days for that small amount of gas to accumulate to lethal levels. Anyway, the thermocouplers on your appliances would detect the absence of a flame and automatically turn off the gas."

The two men looked at her, surprised.

"I interned at the gas company when I was in college," she explained. "It's probably a leak in a line somewhere. Now, put the damn gun away. What are you doing with a gun, anyway?"

"I want to know what he's doing here," David persisted.

Beau, who looked like he'd had enough, suddenly twisted around. In one smooth move he freed his arm from David's grip and had the gun in his hand. "I was just keeping an eye on things.'' He opened the revolver's chamber, emptied the bullets into his hand, and returned the gun to David. ''I hope to hell you have a license for that thing.''

''I do, smart-ass.''

Sirens signaled the arrival of the fire department. The gas company was right on the heels of the fire engine. Soon the mansion was swarming with yellow-coated men and women. The house was aired out, so the danger of an explosion was minimal now.

Aubrey was more worried about her uncle. He was breathing normally, but his face looked gray. She supposed that might be the moonlight. At her insistence, a paramedic looked him over. He gave Wayne some oxygen, and he grudgingly allowed the mask to be put over his face.

Lyle had gone to confer with the firefighters and the gas company people. Aubrey remained sitting on the lawn with her uncle, Beronica, and Carlos. Beau remained with her. She didn't know where David was.

''What were you doing in the bushes?'' she finally asked him. ''Really.''

''Just what I said earlier. I couldn't sleep. I couldn't help thinking that this whole thing is connected to you somehow, at least on the edges. Three brushes with death in two days can't be coincidence. And I wanted to keep an eye on you.''

''Four brushes now,'' Aubrey said, shivering despite the warm temperature. ''What could it mean? I was in the wrong place at the wrong time when I was assaulted at my house. And Cory beating me up—I went looking for trouble. But getting shot at earlier—someone really wants me dead. And now this. I can't believe it's an accident. My God, six people could have died."

He slid his arm around her. "I wasn't much help, either."

"At least your instincts were correct. I thought I'd be safe in my bed, with a cop in the house, the doors and windows and front gate locked."

"A cop in the house?"

"Lyle. He was monitoring the phone."

As if speaking his name had conjured him up, Lyle approached them. He gave Beau a hostile look, then focused on Aubrey. "They found the problem. It was a broken gas line going into the water heater on the second floor. Looks as though mice or rats chewed through it. They repaired it, but you probably should have the whole house inspected. And gas detectors installed."

A guy from the gas company joined them, basically repeating what Lyle had just told them.

Aubrey felt as if a huge weight had been lifted from her shoulders. Rats or mice. It was an accident. No one had tried to kill her or her whole family.

IT WAS ALMOST DAWN by the time things calmed down at the Clarendon mansion. Beau sat on a stone bench by the fountain and watched it all. He was interested in how the Clarendon family related to one another. The gas company had said it was an accident. But how hard would it be to chew through a gas line—with pliers, maybe—and make it look like a rat had done it? A gas leak that almost wiped out an entire family— it was just too much of a coincidence after everything else that had happened. Beau didn't like coincidences. Like Lyle being there just when it happened.

Still, nothing seemed out of whack with the family. David's hostility and his haste in blaming Beau were irritating, but Beau's uninvited presence on the grounds *was* suspicious. He'd have probably done the same thing in David's position, though he'd have done it more skillfully. Taking the .22 away from him had been pathetically easy. David might have a license for the gun, but he hadn't handled weapons much.

Much as he wanted to keep David on the suspect list, he reluctantly scratched him off. From what Aubrey had told him, he'd been instrumental in rescuing Wayne, staying inside the gas-filled house to help the old man down the stairs. Then he'd rescued Beronica and her baby.

But what the hell was Lyle Palmer doing here? Beau understood getting obsessed with a case like this. He could recall some sleepless nights when he'd been a new detective. But manning the Clarendon's tip line wasn't where he should be putting his efforts.

If Lyle had wanted to keep working the case, he should have been out talking to people. Didn't the guy have any informants? He should be finding people who knew Cory. Beau couldn't help feeling Cory was near the center of the mystery. His reaction to Aubrey's curiosity had been so extreme, there was no doubt she'd been sniffing up the right tree. But the bartender–drug dealer had gone to ground. Craig said no one could locate him.

Beau considered the idea that Lyle might have a crush on Aubrey, and thus wanted to stay close to her. That was a motivation he could relate to.

As the gas company cars pulled away, Aubrey joined Beau on the bench. She looked beautiful, with her reddish hair pulled back in a hasty braid, her face milky-pale in the moonlight. She had on the same nightshirt she'd worn the previous morning, pale blue with little clouds on it. He remembered how it had looked as she'd peeled it off.

He stifled a groan. He remembered every detail of their lovemaking as if he'd recorded it digitally in his brain.

"Everyone's going back inside now," she said.

"Is that my cue to get lost?"

"Lyle's so irritated with you he was ready to escort you off the estate at gunpoint. I told him I'd seen quite enough of guns for one night, and that I would talk to you."

"I should get some sleep," he said, but he made no move to leave. "Tell me something. Do you think Lyle has the hots for you?"

"For me?" She looked bewildered. "No. It was Patti he wanted, not me."

"I'm just trying to figure out why he's here. He should have delegated this task to someone else."

"I asked him the same thing. He said he just didn't trust anyone else to handle it right, if the kidnapper called. But I think he's feeling guilty for not jumping on Sara's disappearance with both feet when she first went missing. If anything happens to her, he'll take it very personally."

"I guess I can relate to that." He was here, too, after all. "I wish someone else was in charge. Love him or hate him, he's incompetent."

Aubrey didn't argue.

"So, are you going to kick me off the premises, or what?"

She sighed. "I should. But I won't. The fact is, the only time I feel safe is when I'm with you."

"That's illogical as hell. I haven't done such a hot job protecting you so far."

"What do you mean? You saved me from Cory. And you threw me on the ground when someone was shooting. You kept Charlie from coming in here and killing me."

"But it was pure luck that saved you tonight."

"No, not luck. I heard a baby crying. It woke me up, and it sounded just like Sara. Then I smelled the gas."

"You were probably dreaming."

"I guess. But it seemed so real." Her eyes filled with tears. "Oh, Beau, what if she doesn't come back? What if we just never find her? Maybe Summer wasn't so far off. Maybe someone took Sara, and they're selling her on the black market for an illegal adoption."

He pulled Aubrey close and let her cry on his shoulder. He was amazed she'd held it together this long, after all that had happened today. "We'll find her," he vowed, letting a new determination fill him. It tore him up inside, seeing Aubrey in so much pain.

She put her arms around his neck. "I'm sorry I was so mean to you earlier."

He started to say, *Which time?* Then he stopped himself. She was handing him an olive branch, and he'd be a fool to knock it away. "You've got a lot going on."

"Doesn't excuse me. The truth is, I feel myself...wanting to forgive you. Or at least to believe you still have some good, decent qualities."

"And the love of a good woman could bring them out?" he asked skeptically.

Her laugh turned into a sob. "I'm trying to say something here."

"Sorry." She was talking forgiveness, which was what he'd wanted from her all along. But now, oddly, he felt it wouldn't be enough, having her forgive him for the sins she thought he'd committed. No, he wouldn't be satisfied, he decided, until she understood what had happened that night two years ago.

She ran her index finger along the edge of his black denim vest. "The idea of not hating you scares me."

"It's a lot easier to hate me than to believe Gavin did something really, really wrong."

She stiffened. "He would *never* have shot you. You knew that. He loved you like a brother."

He wanted to tell her the truth. But she obviously wasn't ready to hear it.

"He was a scapegoat, a sacrificial lamb," she continued, gaining momentum. "He was set up, but he was going down, and there was nothing he could do. You should have let him escape."

It sounded almost like a rehearsed speech. How many times had she repeated those words in her head?

"He was guilty, Aubrey."

She pulled away from him. "No! You have to believe that, because it's the only way you can justify what you did. But there is no way Gavin was tampering with evidence."

"He was stealing drugs from the evidence room. Him and a lot of other guys. Those other guys were terrified Gavin would testify against them. Gavin should be glad, real glad, I'm the one who found him."

"You shot him!"

"In the leg. Lots of the cops out there looking for him would have taken a head shot to save their own necks."

"Why didn't you just let him go?" she said, shaking her head. She absolutely refused to consider the possibility Beau was telling the truth.

"Because a couple of years in prison are better than a lifetime as a fugitive."

"You mean ten years."

"He'll be out in two or three. Texas prisons are overcrowded."

That silenced her.

Beau rubbed the back of his hand across his gritty eyes. He really did need to get a couple hours' sleep, or he'd be useless later. And he didn't want to talk about Gavin anymore.

"I'm meeting Craig for lunch tomorrow—today, I mean. He's got a friend who works at the Medical Examiner's office, so he can get the unofficial autopsy report—probably before Palmer hears it."

"How can you even say *lunch* and *autopsy* in the same breath?"

"Sorry." Cops tended to take for granted gruesome crime-scene photos and autopsy reports. He kept forgetting this was Aubrey's cousin they were talking about. "How about if I meet you afterward? You want me to pick you up?"

"The less you show your face around here, the better. I'll meet you. I can borrow a car from Uncle Wayne. Though I need to pick mine up from the motel sometime soon."

"Okay. Stubby's, around two?"

"Not Stubby's." Too many memories. "Melody Lane Park."

"Okay. I've got some other things to show you, but

they can wait.'' He didn't think now was the time to reveal Patti's rap sheet, but it certainly didn't lend credence to Aubrey's belief that Patti had turned her life around.

Chapter Eleven

Melody Lane Park was another place full of youthful memories. Aubrey wasn't sure why she'd picked it—it might be even more painful than Stubby's.

Images floated through her mind...hanging out with a gang of kids, playing touch football in the dark, breath steaming in the wintertime, skin slick with sweat in the summer, like now.

And Beau, always Beau, so close but so untouchable. She'd watched in agony as he went through a succession of girlfriends, and she could never say a word to anyone. Her reluctance had less to do with Gavin and more to do with her abject fear that Beau would reject her or worse, laugh at her, if he knew she had feelings for him. In fact, Gavin's warning was only an excuse she'd used to rationalize her cowardice.

Was she still using Gavin as an excuse? What if she considered the possibility that Beau was telling the truth? That he'd shot Gavin and brought him in not for the money, but to protect him from his own rash actions?

Gavin might be released sooner than she'd thought. And she'd have him back in her life. If he'd fled the country as he'd originally planned, she might not have ever seen him again.

She spotted Beau's Mustang pulling up to the curb near the picnic tables where she waited, and that put an end to her uncomfortable musings. She was surprised to see Craig with him.

She didn't know Craig well. He hadn't hung out at Dudley's as much as some guys because he had a wife and kids to go home to. But he'd seemed nice.

In his mid-thirties, Craig was tall and rangy, his face scarred from a teenage knife fight. But the thin white line that ran from the corner of his eye, down his cheek and over his lip, only gave him a rakish air. Aubrey still thought him handsome, with his unruly, wavy blond hair and twinkling blue eyes.

In twill trousers and a cream-colored silk shirt, he was a sharp contrast walking next to Beau, who wore his ubiquitous black T-shirt, black jeans and motorcycle boots.

She waved to them as they approached. "Hi, Craig, it's nice to see you again."

"Hey, Aubrey, you look good."

That was a gift, she thought. She looked like something the cat dragged in, wearing denim shorts and an oversize Play Golf or Die T-shirt she'd borrowed from David. She hadn't thought about the irony of the slogan till it was too late to change her clothes.

"How's Deena?" she asked Craig, having earlier dredged up the name of his wife.

"She says she's doing a lot better since the divorce."

Aubrey winced. "Sorry. Foot-in-mouth disease. How about the girls?"

He smiled. "They're good."

"So." She looked down at her hands. "You came to deliver the news in person?"

Beau spoke up for the first time. "I thought you'd do better hearing it from Craig than me."

"What?" She leaned forward eagerly. "Is there news about Sara?"

Craig laid a hand on her arm. "No, no. It's just about the autopsy. The M.E. is calling it suicide. Cause of death, asphyxiation from carbon monoxide. No sign of violence, no unusual bruises. Plus, she had a ton of alcohol in her bloodstream."

"Alcohol?" Aubrey shook her head. "That's impossible. Patti didn't drink."

Craig and Beau exchanged a look. "Aubrey," Beau said gently, "I know you want to believe the best of the people you love. But you didn't think Patti was using drugs, either. Or working at a topless bar."

Aubrey started to object, but Craig set a folder in front of her. "This is Patti's rap sheet," he said. "I know this isn't pleasant for you, but you might want to see what's in there."

Aubrey's hand trembled as she opened the folder. And there were all Patti's arrests, listed neatly on a computer printout. Only there were more, far more, than Aubrey had known about.

"Drunk and disorderly? Misdemeanor Possession of an Illegal Substance? Criminal Mischief?" Most of the arrests had occurred more than a year ago, before Sara. But there'd been a couple more recently.

Aubrey read the most recent police reports more closely. Patti had been caught throwing rocks at the windows of a mobile home. Charlie Soffit's trailer. She'd been either drunk or high on drugs, the report said. They'd thrown her in the drunk tank and let her come down. Charlie had declined to press charges.

"The charge is drunk and disorderly," Aubrey said. "But it says here they *let her come down*. She wasn't drunk, she was high on methamphetamines. That was her drug of choice. She never smoked grass, she never snorted coke. She smoked crystal meth."

"She might have gotten drunk to give herself false courage before she killed herself," Beau said. "Maybe she couldn't get her hands on the drug she preferred."

"She was allergic to alcohol," Aubrey insisted. "A few sips of a wine cooler, and five minutes later she was throwing up uncontrollably. There is no way in hell she would willingly drink alcohol. Someone was forcing her."

Craig and Beau exchanged another look.

"There was no sign of—"

"Whoever did this wouldn't need violence!" Aubrey exploded. "They had Sara. No matter what this computer printout says, she loved her daughter. She'd have died for her baby. And apparently that's what she did."

Craig's cell phone rang, as if punctuating Aubrey's proclamation. He answered it, then walked a few feet away for privacy. Beau said nothing.

"You know what I'm saying makes sense," she said, trying to calm herself. No one listened to hysterical females. "Maybe I had blinders on where Patti's concerned. Maybe I did want to believe the best about her. But she would not have gotten drunk. Whoever staged that little scene at the roadside park obviously didn't know she had the allergy.

"And even if she did kill herself, she would have seen to Sara's safety first. If you're thinking she left

Sara in a garbage can or something horrible like that, just stop thinking it. She would have given Sara to me.''

"She did call you and beg you to come home."

"She would have left a note. At the very least, she would have implicated Cory before she died. It's not like Patti to just quietly kill herself in some anonymous park."

"People do strange things—"

"Beau, you can't say anything that will make me accept this ruling."

"I know. You're nothing, Aubrey, if not blindly loyal. There are worse qualities," he added, as if that made it better that he didn't believe her.

She started to object, then clamped her mouth shut. He was right. She'd refused to believe her brother did anything wrong, despite lots of evidence to the contrary. And now she was doing it again.

Craig returned, sticking his cell phone in his pants pocket. "Bad news. They've released Charlie Soffit."

"What?" Beau and Aubrey said together.

"The swabs on his hands came back negative, and his gun didn't match up to the bullet or the shell casings. He didn't fire that shot at you."

"What about the bite mark on his arm?"

"They had a doctor examine the wound. He couldn't say whether it was a dog or human bite."

"But Charlie threatened to kill me!"

"People say crazy things when they're drunk, and in the throes of grief. They did charge him with drunk driving, but he posted a bond for that."

"Grief? Oh, come on."

"We've been checking around with his friends and family," Craig said, "It seems he really did want to marry Patti. She's the one who left him, and she wanted him out of her life. Also, before this incident, he was never even arrested.''

Aubrey put her head in her hands. She couldn't continue to argue with the avalanche of evidence in her face. ''Did I know Patti at all? Was she just using me because I put a free roof over her head and I was a handy baby-sitter? She told me Charlie was an ex-con. I must be the most gullible person on earth.''

Beau moved around the picnic table to sit beside her. ''I don't think your instincts about Patti were all wrong. She *was* trying to turn her life around, for Sara's sake. She had a legitimate job. She was trying to pay off her drug debt so she could put that part of her life behind her. She was trying to be a responsible mother. But people don't change a hundred-and-eighty degrees overnight. She backslid a little, that's all. And if she lied to you, it was probably to protect you. Don't automatically assume she didn't love you.''

She reached over and squeezed his hand. ''Thank you, Beau. I guess I tend to see things in black and white, and Patti was definitely shades of gray. If we could just find Sara,'' she added, ''I'd handle the rest of this a lot better.''

Beau squeezed back. ''We'll find her.''

But it was getting harder and harder for Aubrey to believe that.

PATTI'S FUNERAL WAS the following day. David had made the arrangements as quickly as possible after her body was released from the county medical examiner's office. ''Best to get it over with,'' he'd said. ''For Dad's sake. He insists on attending, though I can't imagine the heat will be good for him.''

There had been no more significant leads as to Sara's whereabouts, and Aubrey sensed an air of pessimism drifting over the cops she talked to, including Lyle. Sara had been missing for three days now. If a kidnapper wanted to ransom her, he'd have made contact by now. They had no fresh leads. Charlie Soffit was still a suspect, because he didn't have a solid alibi for the afternoon Sara had disappeared. Then again, the time of her disappearance was so foggy, almost no one could come up with an alibi. She could have been taken any time between Patti's phone call to Aubrey on Tuesday morning and her death late that afternoon, though even her time of death couldn't be accurately pinpointed.

But the police had investigated Charlie pretty thoroughly. They'd searched his trailer, talked to his friends and relatives, and they hadn't found a shred of evidence indicating his involvement.

Cory was still missing, and he was considered a "person of interest," since Patti was apparently fleeing from him the day she died. His disappearance was suspicious, to say the least. But Patti wouldn't have willingly given Sara to such a creep. And if he'd taken Sara forcibly, Patti would have gone to the cops, never mind that she hated cops. She wouldn't have just meekly driven off to a park and killed herself.

The prevailing theory was still that Patti had left her baby somewhere, or with someone, she thought would be safe. And whoever had her now, for whatever reason, was afraid to come forward.

Aubrey hoped that was the truth.

Since Aubrey had no clothes with her suitable for a funeral, she had to go home. So Beau picked her up at her uncle's house the morning of the funeral, took her to get her car, then followed her back to her house.

Beau went in first. With his gun in hand, he checked every room and every closet to make sure it was safe. Only then did he allow Aubrey inside. A few days ago she would have considered this excessive caution. Not now.

Aubrey took her small duffel bag upstairs, emptied her dirty clothes into the hamper, then pulled clothes haphazardly out of her drawers and repacked—enough to last three or four days. She intended to stay at her uncle's house as long as he wanted her there, as long as she was serving some half-useful function in the search for Sara. Beau agreed her home wouldn't be safe until both Sara and Cory were found and the mystery unraveled. The perpetrator obviously thought Aubrey either knew something or had seen something that could implicate him, and that was why she'd become a target.

But Aubrey had gone over and over in her mind everything she knew about Patti's life, and Patti had told her precious little that would implicate anyone. Nothing about Cory, nothing about Greg Holmes's shady insurance practices or his extramarital activities. Who else hadn't she told Aubrey about?

Aubrey put on the only clothes she owned appropriate for a funeral, a navy skirt and a subdued gray silk shell. She managed to locate some serviceable navy pumps and one good pair of panty hose. She hated the thought of wearing stockings in this heat, but her parents had come up from South Padre for the funeral, and her mother would lecture her for years if she went bare-legged to a funeral.

She pulled her unruly hair back into a twist, secured

with a silver comb, then added a minimum of makeup. She stopped herself before she could spritz on perfume. She was primping for Beau.

"I'm sorry, Patti," she murmured. She was ashamed for letting her hormones dictate her behavior at a time like this. Then again, Patti probably would have been amused. She always thought Aubrey was a dud when it came to men, that if only she'd try a little harder, wear sexier clothes and walk with her chest out, she'd have all the boyfriends she wanted.

"Well, Patti, I've got a live one now," she said, changing her mind and putting just a tiny bit of scent on her wrists. But she wasn't quite sure what to do with him. The idea of putting aside the past and exploring a relationship with Beau seemed insane. How could she possibly get involved with the man who'd shot her brother? She imagined introducing him to friends and colleagues. *This is my boyfriend, Beau Maddox. Yes, that's right. The one who shot Gavin.* Even worse, how would she explain it to her parents? Or to Gavin himself?

But deep down, she knew she'd been holding on to an idealized version of her brother's crime, his flight to avoid prosecution, and his capture. The testimony Beau had given in court had made perfect sense. All she had to do was allow herself to believe it, and the barriers between her and Beau would melt away. Was she ready for that?

When she came downstairs and saw the purely male appreciation in his eyes, she wanted nothing better than to let him take her upstairs and peel off all the clothes she'd just put on.

He didn't look half-bad himself, she realized. Though he still wore black jeans, he'd traded the black pocket T-shirt for a gray one. The biker vest and boots were gone, replaced by a black leather blazer and black dress boots.

"That jacket is going to be hot," she said.

"I have to wear something to conceal the gun."

She should be used to that by now, considering how long she'd been around cops. But it still startled her.

Beau drove her back to her uncle's house. He insisted on following the limousine to the cemetery, where they would have a simple graveside service. Besides wanting to see who showed up at the funeral, which could be very illuminating, he wanted to stay close to Aubrey in case of trouble.

The limousine was actually chilly inside. Aubrey's uncle sat across from her. His dark suit, once expertly tailored to his robust form, now hung on him like laundry on a clothesline. She was worried about him, but Mary, the hospice nurse, had paid him a visit this morning and had declared him well enough to make it through the funeral.

David sat next to Uncle Wayne, dashing in a navy suit. He had a small shaving nick on his chin, which made him seem very young all of a sudden, younger than her. His face was grim, his mouth set in a thin line. But he tapped his fingers on his knee in a nervous rhythm, and he couldn't seem to sit still.

He'd brought a briefcase with him, which he'd slid under the seat. "What the hell is that for?" Wayne asked.

"Some papers for Jim. I've been doing a little work at home." Jim was one of the partners at the law firm.

"You don't do business during a funeral." Wayne sounded outraged.

"I'm not doing business. I'm just giving him the

papers. The client needs them, and the reputation of the firm shouldn't suffer because of our personal crises.''

"Jim's coming to the house later," Wayne grumbled. He didn't like to be contradicted. "You could have done it then."

David gave his dad a rueful grin. "You're right. My brain hasn't been working straight lately."

Aubrey's parents sat next to her. They'd arrived late last night and had said little. They hadn't been terribly pleased when Aubrey had taken Patti in. Her mother, Ginger, had feared Patti would bring trouble with her—and, boy, had she been right. To Ginger's credit, though, she'd been nothing but supportive since her arrival.

"I never expected Patti to kill herself," Wayne said suddenly. David's nervous finger-tapping stopped. "She was wild and melodramatic," Wayne continued, "but if someone had pushed her to the end of her tether, I'd have expected her to commit murder, not suicide."

"I don't imagine she wanted to go to jail," David said. "She didn't like it much the first time she was there."

"Well, she wouldn't plan on getting caught," Wayne said, almost smiling. "She always thought she could get away with things. And if she *were* going to kill herself," he continued, "don't you think she'd make a big production out of it? Shoot herself on the evening news, perhaps? But she did it in a roadside park, where perhaps she wouldn't have been found for days. It's not like her."

Aubrey had been troubled by the same thoughts. But no one would listen to what she had to say. Patti's allergy to alcohol hadn't impressed Lyle at all. "If she was going to die anyway," he'd said a trifle impatiently, "do you think she'd care about a little nausea?"

Aubrey had thought Lyle's attitude callous. Earlier he'd said he felt guilty for not launching a more energetic investigation from the beginning, but sometimes he didn't act guilty at all. He acted mean. When the funeral was over, she decided she would see if she could get Lyle removed from the case. Her uncle probably had enough clout to do it. That meant a new investigator would have to start all over, but maybe he'd be more competent than Lyle Palmer.

The service started at ten, so it wasn't too awfully hot yet. And the Clarendon family plot, in the old part of the city cemetery, was shaded by huge black oak trees. Aubrey was amazed at the number of people there. Some of them were reporters, she realized. She wanted to scream at them that they shouldn't intrude on this private time. But the media vultures were her allies for the moment, keeping the story of Sara's disappearance in the public consciousness, so she had to be nice to them.

Some of the people standing around were undoubtedly curiosity seekers, too. Wayne Clarendon was as close to a public figure as Payton, Texas, had, and the suicide-kidnapping intrigued the townspeople.

As the family got out of the limousine, Beau was instantly beside them. He said hello to Aubrey's parents. Aubrey tensed, praying there wouldn't be a scene. Her parents had been furious with Beau after Gavin's shooting, almost as mad as Aubrey. But they were polite now, and Aubrey's mother even gave Beau a little shoulder squeeze.

Beau stuck close to Aubrey as they all sat down in the white folding chairs on the row reserved for family. He sat next to her without apology.

"The person who wants to hurt you is still out there somewhere," he murmured. She hadn't told her parents everything, so she was glad they couldn't overhear. "A funeral might be a good opportunity for a sniper." He looked around again. "Who are all these people?"

Aubrey identified the ones she could. "Those three older men over there? They're the partners in Wayne's law firm. Jim Thomason is the older one. Not sure of the names of the other two.

"That family, the man and woman and two teenage boys, are distant cousins on my mother's side. I haven't talked to them in years, but Patti used to baby-sit for them. The woman—" She stopped, her attention snagged by a man and woman climbing out of a red Cadillac.

"Greg Holmes," Beau said, apparently having spotted them at the same time. "And Summer. Guess it's only appropriate Patti's employer put in an appearance."

"He's been wearing long sleeves every time we've seen him," Aubrey said, just realizing it. "I'd love to look at his right arm."

"Summer looks like she's enjoying this," Beau commented. The flamboyant young woman wore a tight black dress, too low-cut and too short for a funeral. Greg had his arm around her as if to comfort her. As they found two chairs toward the front, Summer seemed to break down weeping. Greg offered her his handkerchief.

"I must ask Summer what brand of eye makeup she uses," Aubrey said dryly. "It doesn't smear at all."

Greg dabbed at his own dry eyes before pocketing the hanky.

"Oh, nice touch," Beau said. "Quite the thespians, that pair."

"Have you found out anything about them?" Aubrey asked.

"Craig went to the guys in Fraud. They already had a bead on Holmes. In fact, they'd interviewed Patti."

"Really?" This seemed like a promising lead.

"According to the detective on the case, Patti didn't tell them anything. He seemed to think she really didn't know much."

"Or she was protecting her lover," Aubrey said. "Patti was quite the actress herself. Hey, maybe he thought she was going to turn on him," Aubrey whispered excitedly. "If he tried to end the affair, for example. Or, more likely, if she was blackmailing him. She did need money, after all. Does he have an alibi for Monday afternoon?"

"He and Summer alibi'd each other."

"For what that's worth. Do you know if Lyle considers either of them suspects? He's not exactly forthcoming with me."

"Craig says Palmer is finally focused on Cory. The manhunt has gotten pretty intensive."

"It's about time. Cory is completely crazy." Aubrey shivered as she remembered the maniacal look in Cory's eyes as he'd wielded the whip, really enjoying her pain. But there'd been a sense of desperation about him, too. He'd apparently thought Aubrey was much closer to incriminating him than she was.

A small cadre of cops arrived next in an unmarked

sedan, so bland it almost screamed "cop car." Lyle was in the lead. The others—one woman in plain clothes, and two uniforms—Aubrey didn't recognize.

She hoped Lyle wouldn't come forward to offer his condolences. She just wasn't feeling charitable toward him right now.

"Oh, my God, will you look at that."

Aubrey looked where Beau nodded. She saw a man in an ill-fitting suit climbing off a motorcycle. It took her several heartbeats to recognize the newcomer as Charlie Soffit. In addition to the new clothes, he'd gotten a haircut and a shave. And he looked dead sober.

"You know, he cleans up pretty nice," Aubrey said. "He's almost handsome."

Charlie didn't make his way to the front, but instead hung back behind the other mourners, near the trunk of a tree, almost as if he didn't want to be noticed. His face was a mask of sorrow, his eyes a bit puffy. Unlike Greg's and Summer's crocodile tears, Charlie's looked real.

Aubrey pointed out a few other people—innocuous neighbors, a couple of Patti's school friends she probably hadn't seen in years, the elderly pediatrician who'd treated all the Schuyler and Clarendon kids when they'd been growing up.

A minister stood up before the assemblage, and the hushed conversations ceased. "It's difficult to know what to say at any funeral," he began, "but doubly difficult when the deceased is so young...."

He droned on, but Aubrey had a hard time paying attention. She found herself listening to a whispered conversation in the row behind her, where the law firm partners were sitting. She could only catch a few words here and there, but they were enough to disturb her.

"…acting strangely before his sister…"

"…not fooling anyone…"

"How much do you suppose he paid for…"

"*I* can't afford a Porsche."

"…talk to Wayne—today."

"…tired of his runaround…"

"…talked to the accountant. No way to explain…"

Aubrey nudged Beau in the ribs. "Can you hear that?" she whispered in his ear, trying not to think about how good he smelled. She'd never known him to wear aftershave before.

"Hear what?"

"What those guys behind us are talking about?"

He shook his head.

Aubrey strained her ears to hear more. She'd always had good hearing, probably because she hadn't indulged in the loud rock music most of her friends had favored.

"Now is not the time." That was definitely Jim's voice.

"If we wait, it might be too late."

"It might just finish the old guy off."

Aubrey felt a note of alarm. They were talking about Wayne. They had some upsetting news to give him, and it concerned David—and money.

She thought about what Wayne had said the other day regarding David: *He always did have a strange attitude about money. It's never been something that worried him, anyway.*

Well, maybe David didn't worry about money, but the partners sounded almost frantic. Maybe they didn't want David as a partner. That would certainly have an impact on David's finances, and it would greatly upset Wayne.

She didn't want to think about that now, though. She was supposed to be mourning for Patti—and watching the other mourners for suspicious behavior.

"Look over there," Beau whispered. "To the right."

A couple of real strange characters had sidled up, a young man and woman, wearing lots of leather, studs and chains. Their costumes made Summer look appropriate for tea with the queen.

"People she knew from Kink," Aubrey said, waving away a mosquito. Darn perfume. "I think the woman is a waitress there. Let's talk to them after the service."

"They'll be gone after the service," Beau said, slipping out of his chair.

The minister's gaze flickered toward Beau, but his words of comfort never faltered. The rather generic eulogy was winding to an end, and people were growing restless.

Aubrey heard a cell phone. *How irritating,* she thought. Then she realized it was David's phone. She was going to give him hell later for this. He answered it as everyone stood up. By prearrangement, the family was supposed to throw a little bit of dirt on the casket as it was lowered into the ground. She hated this tradition. She didn't want to focus on Patti being laid to rest in the cold ground.

Aubrey led the way out of the front row of chairs. She walked up to stand by the grave as the pallbearers, assisted by a couple of guys from the cemetery, lowered the casket into the grave.

But where was David? He was one of the pallbearers. Aubrey looked around and finally spotted her cousin walking away from the crowd, still talking on his cell phone.

What? What phone call could be more important than his own sister's last moments above ground?

Chapter Twelve

Beau stood by the massive trunk of an oak tree, watching David's retreat. He caught Aubrey's eye and motioned for her to join him.

"I'll be right back," she whispered to her mother.

"What? Aubrey…"

But she didn't have time to explain. David's behavior was damned odd, and she had a strong feeling that whatever was going on with him, she and Beau needed to know.

"What's he doing?" Beau demanded.

"I don't know. He got a call on his cell and he took off."

He was heading for the limousine.

Beau and Aubrey took out after him at a brisk walk. "David," she called out. "Wait!"

"I'll be right back," David called over his shoulder.

"The hell," Beau muttered, breaking into a run, leaving Aubrey to catch up. But David had too much of a lead on him. He hopped into the limousine's driver's seat, then drove off like a shot. The uniformed driver, who'd been loitering nearby smoking a cigarette, could do nothing but stare in disbelief.

"I have to follow him," Beau said to Aubrey. "You

have to come with me. I'm not leaving you here without protection.''

She wouldn't have let him leave without her, anyway. She was dying of curiosity. What was David up to? Was he trying to avoid a confrontation with the partners? Did he want to be absent when the partners told Wayne whatever the big secret was?

She and Beau jumped into Beau's Mustang, but he didn't take off right away. He let the limo get a good head start.

''He's getting away!'' Aubrey cried.

''No, he's not. I just don't want him to know I'm following. Get out your phone. Call First Strike. See if anyone's there.'' He rattled off the number, but he had to repeat it because her fingers were shaking.

Lori Bettencourt answered. Aubrey gave the phone to Beau. ''Lori. Is anyone there? I need help with a tail.'' He paused, then continued. ''Rex. There's a black limousine headed south on—yes, that's right, a limo. He's turning west on Briar, near—hell, I don't know.''

''Augustine,'' Aubrey provided.

''Okay, on channel 30.'' He hung up the phone and turned on his CB.

''I didn't know anyone still used those,'' Aubrey said.

''Us and the truckers. I hate cell phones. They cut out at the worst moments.''

''Who's Rex?'' Aubrey asked.

''Rex Bettencourt. Lori's big brother. Ex–Special Forces. Good guy to have on your side. Listen, what were those men behind us talking about?''

''Oh. Something about David and mishandling of funds or something. They weren't happy with him, at any rate. Maybe it had something to do with how he raised the cash for the ransom. I couldn't get the whole story. But Wayne gave David carte blanche to do whatever it took to raise a million dollars.''

''I hope that's all it is.''

''Why do you say that?''

''The cops did an investigation into David's background—yours and Wayne's, too.''

''What?''

''It's purely routine. To rule all of you out as suspects. They didn't find anything criminal, but they did discover that David had an obscene amount of debt.''

Further discussion of David's finances was cut short when a man's voice came over the radio. ''I'm here. What's your twenty?''

Beau grabbed the mike. ''I'm crossing Augustine now. The limo is a couple of blocks ahead of me. We've got a few cars between us now.''

''I'll be there in about three minutes.''

''From First Strike?'' Aubrey asked, alarmed. The agency was six or seven miles away.

''Don't underestimate Rex Bettencourt's driving. He makes me look like a little old lady. Keep an eye out for him. He's in a black Bronco.'' Then he spoke into the mike again. ''Looks like our friend is getting on the freeway, going…north.''

''I got a visual,'' Rex said. ''Nice wheels. What's going on?''

''I don't know. That's what I want to find out. I'll try to get ahead of him.''

Beau treated Aubrey to a hair-raising tour of back streets and farm-to-market roads that weren't designed for such speed. She double-checked her seat belt, then scrunched her eyes closed. "I'm getting on at FM 1322," Beau told Rex.

"You should be a good fifty yards ahead of us. I'll peel off."

Sure enough, Aubrey saw the limo in their rearview mirror. A black Bronco, a few car lengths behind it, took an exit. Beau slowed to sixty and cruised in the right lane, a comfortable distance ahead of the limo.

"He's signaling," Aubrey said.

Beau grabbed the radio. "He's getting off at the Faircroft exit."

Aubrey felt sick to her stomach. "The rest stop, where they found Patti…"

"Yeah, it's right around here. I had a look at it yesterday." Beau took the next exit and got in the U-turn lane. "It winds back well away from the access road, and it's overgrown with vegetation. A good place to commit a crime."

"Oh, Beau, what if David is heading right into a trap? I can't help but think he wouldn't leave Patti's funeral like this unless it was a matter of life and death." She recalled his show of nerves in the limo earlier. "He had a briefcase with him," she suddenly remembered. "Oh, you don't think—"

Beau cursed softly. "He's paying a ransom. No doubt in my mind. Someone told him not to involve the cops, and he didn't."

"Then he really might be in danger. Whoever it is might not even have Sara."

Beau got on the radio. "Proceed with extreme caution. Our subject is meeting with someone who might be very dangerous."

"10-4."

"Should I call 911?" Aubrey asked.

"Cops won't get here in time. Anyway, a big show of sirens might scare this guy off."

"Better that than having him hurt David."

"Trust me, David is more likely to get hurt if they think he led the cops to them. Let me do this my way, okay?"

Aubrey gulped. "Okay." *Please,* she prayed, *don't let this have anything to do with the reward.* If Beau didn't want to involve the cops because he wanted to make sure he got the reward, she wouldn't be able to stand it.

She'd only recently come to believe that Beau might be telling the truth about how and why he shot Gavin. And as she'd allowed that possibility to creep into her consciousness, all her carefully constructed, rigorously guarded animosity toward Beau was evaporating like rain on a hot Texas day.

He'd wiggled his way into her heart.

No, it was more than that. She was stunned to realize she'd fallen in love with the guy. Not the puppy love or hero worship of her past, but the deep, enduring kind of love that came only when she could accept him, all of him, the good and the bad. And if the bad included a sinister motive for his current behavior, it would tear her apart.

This was a hell of a time to realize she loved him, when he might be about to get his head shot off.

"He's turning into the rest stop," Rex said over the radio, dragging Aubrey back to the present.

"Don't let him see you."

"What kind of a bounty hunter do you think I am?"

Just when Aubrey saw the sign for the rest stop a hundred feet ahead, Beau pulled off the road almost into a ditch. She saw the black Bronco. Was black the mandatory color for bounty hunters' cars? she wondered.

Rex Bettencourt stood on the hood of the Bronco, peering through binoculars. Aubrey's initial impression of him had been that he was *big, solid and scary.* Now she realized how truly tall he was, maybe six foot three. He sported a couple of days' growth of blond beard on his lean, tanned face.

He wore khaki pants and a camouflage flak vest, and the biggest brown boots she'd ever seen. He could do some damage with those things.

Beau reached into the glove box and grabbed a box of ammunition, then climbed out. He'd seemingly forgotten Aubrey, so she quietly got out, too. This seemed a safe enough vantage point.

"I can just barely see where the limo stopped," Rex said. "So far no one's gotten in or out. I don't see any other people or vehicles, but there's ample places to hide either."

"Let's move in. You take the north, I'll take the south. The ditch, and then that little ridge, should provide us with plenty of cover."

"What's our objective?"

"Keep the guy in the limo safe. Second objective is to apprehend whoever he's meeting. And if you see any sign of a baby—"

"Enough said," Rex replied as he climbed down from the hood of the Bronco.

"What should I—" Aubrey began, but Beau didn't even let her finish the question.

He pointed at her, his expression fierce. "You get back in the car. If you hear shots, then you can call the cops."

His command was so authoritative, Aubrey obeyed

it. At first. But she'd seen something in the Mustang's glove box that intrigued her. She opened it. Yes, that was what she thought. Another gun, a small revolver.

She knew a little bit about guns. When Gavin and Beau had first joined the force, Gavin had thought she ought to learn about firearms. So he'd taken her to the shooting range and taught her the basics. She'd resolutely refused to get a gun of her own, figuring that in a pinch she'd forget how to use it and the bad guy would take it away from her and shoot her. Beau had agreed that, if she felt that way, she shouldn't have a gun.

But now she was in a pinch, and she didn't feel apprehensive at all. She took the .22 from the glove box and checked the cylinder. It was fully loaded.

She followed Beau's trail, not too difficult since he'd been practically wading through tall weeds. She cursed her inappropriate attire—pumps weren't the best shoes for trekking cross-country, and brambles were shredding her nylons, not to mention what was happening to her bare arms. But she pressed on, the gun in her right hand, the cell phone in her left.

Maybe she wasn't a crack shot, she reasoned, but surely one more gun on the good guys' side was better than nothing. She couldn't bear it if anything happened to David.

She pushed her way through a stand of cattails and realized she'd almost reached the open. The limo was just a few feet away, the engine idling. Maybe she should remain here, where weeds hid her from view.

Then again, the weeds weren't much protection if bullets started flying.

She was considering her alternatives when a hand clamped over her mouth from behind. Her gun hand was pinned against her body. She was unceremoniously jerked to the ground and dragged behind a concrete culvert, where she found herself sitting in a puddle of slimy water.

About that time she realized her assailant was Beau.

"What the hell do you think you're doing?" he hissed.

"Providing backup," she said when he removed his hand from her mouth.

He took the gun away from her with amazing ease and tucked it into the back of his jeans. "God help us."

"What? I know how to shoot."

"One lesson at a firing range does not qualify you—" He stopped, jerked his head up. Aubrey could have sworn he sniffed the air. "Don't move a hair," he said, "or so help me I'll shoot you myself."

Her knight in shining armor.

As her heartbeat returned to something like normal, she peeked over the culvert and tried to see what had snagged his attention. The vegetation on the opposite side of the narrow lane where the limo was parked had moved. It moved again.

The limo door opened and David got out. He was holding the briefcase.

David! She screamed mentally. *Don't make yourself a target.* But no one fired at him.

The bushes wiggled again, and a man emerged. It took Aubrey all of two seconds to recognize him. Just the sight of him caused a shiver of revulsion to shimmy up her spine.

"It's Cory." She hardly breathed the words.

"I know."

"What are you waiting for? Do something. Shoot him."

"I can't shoot an unarmed man."

Oh, right. Those super ethics. She had to bite her tongue to keep from saying it aloud. First Strike indeed. "Can't you come up behind him? Disarm him?"

"I'm hoping Rex is in position behind him," Beau said, never taking his gaze off the two men near the limo. "But if we take Cory now, he might not lead us to Sara."

"Do you think he has Sara?" she asked hopefully.

He didn't answer. David and Cory, standing a few feet apart, were talking in voices too low to carry. Cory made a gesture like, *Hey, I'm a nice guy. You can trust me.*

She hoped David wouldn't trust him. Cory reached for the briefcase, then froze. That was when Aubrey realized David was the one with the gun.

"Oh, Christ," Beau muttered.

There was more talk. More negotiating, it looked like. David opened the briefcase, fumbling as he tried to keep the gun trained on Cory. Aubrey realized he was leaving himself vulnerable. But Cory didn't try to take the gun away. He seemed too interested in the contents of the briefcase.

Aubrey couldn't see inside, but she assumed it contained great wads of cash, because Cory smiled and nodded with satisfaction. Both men relaxed their stances slightly. David pointed his gun toward the ground.

To her surprise, Cory turned and disappeared once again into the vegetation.

"What's he doing?" Aubrey whispered. "Do you think Rex will be able to catch him?"

"Shh. If Rex wants to catch him, he will. But I hope he doesn't. Not if Cory is going where I think he's going."

"Where?"

Beau didn't answer. They watched in tense silence as David waited. Aubrey became intensely aware of her wet clothes and the terrible smell of stagnant water, trash, and dead things the recent rain had no doubt washed to this area. Bugs started to bite her, but she couldn't even slap them away for fear the movement or noise would alert Cory to their presence.

She heard a rustling noise nearby and almost fainted when she saw a snake about ten feet away, moving through some weeds. She tapped Beau on the arm and pointed frantically at the slithering reptile as it approached.

He looked, then shrugged and returned to his vigil. "It's a harmless racer, probably more scared of us than we are of him."

Aubrey didn't think that was possible, as her heart was already trying to pound its way out of her chest and she'd broken out in a cold sweat. But when she threw a stick at the snake, it froze for several long seconds, then turned and headed back the way it had come.

Aubrey allowed herself to breathe. She returned her attention to David and the limo just as Cory emerged from the trees again. And when Aubrey realized what was dangling from one hand, she almost cried out with joy.

Cory was carrying a child's car seat. Sara's car seat. And though she couldn't see what was inside, as it was bundled up in blankets, she could only pray it was really Sara, safe and sound.

Cory set the child seat on the ground and stepped away from it. David did the same with the briefcase.

"Make sure it's really Sara," Beau murmured.

Then Aubrey realized that David might not be able to recognize his niece. He hadn't seen her in months, and babies her age changed quickly.

Cory darted forward, grabbed the briefcase, and hightailed it into the woods. Beau reacted instantly.

"Stay here!" he ordered Aubrey. "I'm going after him."

He ran into the open, but he managed to stay behind David, and his footsteps made no sound. How did he do that? Aubrey wondered. Then he ducked behind the limo. David never saw him.

David reached into the car seat and pulled the blankets back. The baby—and yes, it was definitely a baby—cried, and Aubrey knew it was Sara. And she absolutely couldn't stay hidden in the disgusting culvert any longer. Her baby—Sara was hers now—was crying, and she needed comfort. David, clueless male that he was, just squatted down, staring at the baby as if it were a space alien.

Aubrey climbed out of the culvert. "David?"

David whirled around, and she realized too late the gun was still in his hand. She ducked and covered her head, for all the good it would do.

"Don't shoot, it's me, Aubrey!"

He didn't shoot. He ran over to her and helped her to her feet. "Aubrey, what are you doing here?"

But Aubrey had no time for explanations now. She had tunnel vision for that baby, who was now squalling mad. Aubrey ran to her, unbuckled the safety strap and drew the baby out of her car seat. She held Sara out at arm's length, trying to see if there were any injuries.

"Is she okay?" David asked.

Sara's little yellow romper and matching T-shirt were filthy and it looked as if her diaper hadn't been changed in a long while, but there weren't any obvious injuries. "I think so. But we better take her to a hospital."

"What are you doing here?" David asked again. "Where's your car?"

"I came with Beau. We followed you from the cemetery. He went after Cory."

David sagged against the limo. "Oh, hell, Aubrey, why couldn't you just let me do this? I wasn't supposed to involve anyone else. That guy—Cory, you said?—promised he'd kill me if anyone came after him."

"He's already wanted. He's the one who assaulted me at least once, probably twice."

"You mean he's that drug dealer?"

"Yeah." She hugged Sara to her, and the baby quieted and began sucking her thumb. "We can sort all this out later. Right now, I think we should get Sara checked out by a doctor. But I don't want to just leave Beau and Rex out there in the woods. What if something happens to them?"

"Who's Rex?"

"Another bounty hunter."

"Nice company you're keeping." But then David put his arms around both her and Sara. "I'm sorry I almost shot you. You scared me to death."

"*I* scared *you?*"

A rustling in the woods halted their conversation. David gallantly placed his body in front of Aubrey and

Sara, and the gun appeared in his hand again. But it was Beau, winded and a little worse for wear. He had a scratch oozing blood across his cheek and nose.

"He got away," Beau said, still breathing hard. "He had a car parked just on the other side of this hill. He got to it before I could catch him. Is that Sara? Is she okay?"

"We think so," Aubrey said. "But we need to take her to the hospital."

"I need to stay here and hook up with Rex," he said. He looked at Aubrey. "Call the cops. Bring them up to speed. Cory fled in a white Firebird with a red pinstripe. The license plate had been removed."

David stuck out his hand to Beau. "Thanks for trying, man."

Beau shook the proffered hand, but Aubrey thought his eyes looked angry. "You shouldn't have done this on your own."

"Hey, I got Sara back, didn't I? What was I supposed to do? He said he'd kill Sara if I let the cops know. I couldn't risk it. Wayne has a lot more money than he has grandchildren."

Aubrey wasn't a hundred percent sure she wouldn't have done the same thing in David's place. She said an uneasy goodbye to Beau. Then she buckled Sara into the back seat of the limo and climbed in beside her. As David got the limo underway, she got on her cell phone and tried to explain the recent turn of events to the first detective she got on the line. Unfortunately, the ones most familiar with the case were at the funeral.

Pandemonium reigned at Baptist Medical Center where they took Sara. It seemed as if the whole police department was there. They had evidence people who would take charge of Sara's clothing and car seat and comb them for trace evidence. Several uniforms kept the public and the press at bay. And a group of detectives each took David and Aubrey to separate rooms to question them.

Aubrey knew it was standard procedure. The cops had to make sure that Sara's sudden reappearance wasn't the result of some scheme between the two cousins to defraud Wayne Clarendon out of a million dollars—which, it turns out, was the amount Cory demanded, based on the reward offered, and the amount David had given him. But she still resented being treated like a suspect. But cops, she knew, did not appreciate being left out, and they didn't hold back their frustration and disapproval.

Still, she told herself to just let it wash over her. Sara was back, she was safe—a nurse told her the baby had been hungry and thirsty but otherwise fine.

The whole ordeal took several hours, after which Aubrey was not a little hungry and thirsty herself. A couple of cups of hospital coffee hadn't done much but make her stomach burn. But finally—finally—Sara was turned over to Aubrey's care. She guessed hers and David's stories had meshed close enough that the cops didn't suspect them of anything.

Everyone gathered at the Clarendon home, a little later than planned, but Beronica had prepared plenty of food. What had been anticipated as a somber occasion took on a slightly festive atmosphere, due to everyone's joy over baby Sara's return. The baby got passed from relative to friend to relative, everyone anxious to hold the baby and feel her solid little body and be reassured that she actually was fine.

Aubrey silently apologized to Patti for the high spirits, but she figured Patti would be happy, too, that her baby was safe.

Lyle Palmer, who'd been strutting around as if he'd had something to do with Sara's return, took Aubrey aside to the library once people started leaving and the media frenzy was abating.

"So, where's Maddox?" he asked casually.

Aubrey shrugged, trying to act casual herself. But Beau's continued absence was puzzling. "I don't know. He said he had to hook up with Rex, who was presumably still in the woods somewhere."

"Since he's not entitled to any reward, do you think he's washed his hands of the whole case?"

"Well, the case is solved. I guess he doesn't have any reason to hang around." *Except for me.* But he no doubt had wanted to avoid the throngs of cops at the hospital and here, at the house. It had to be really awkward for him to interact with his former co-workers, all of whom felt strongly about him, one way or another. Many of them thought he'd betrayed them by turning Gavin in, though in the end Gavin's testimony hadn't put anyone but himself behind bars.

She tried to tell herself that was why Beau stayed away now. She didn't want to believe it was because, with the reward a moot point, he no longer wanted to spend time with her.

"Do you believe he was telling the truth?" Lyle asked. "That Cory got away?"

"Of course I do."

"You don't think it's barely possible that Maddox and his cohort...Rex, did you say?"

"Yes, Rex Bettencourt," she repeated for the umpteenth time. Hell, Lyle knew perfectly well who it was.

"You don't think it's barely possible that Maddox

and Rex Bettencourt caught up with Cory in the woods, killed him or left him for dead, and took his briefcase?''

''That's preposterous. They're bounty hunters. Not cold-blooded killers.''

''A million dollars could turn just about anyone into a killer. And Rex Bettencourt, former Special Forces, mind you, *is* a killer.''

''I can't speak for Rex, I don't know him. But Beau Maddox would not do what you're suggesting.''

''Hell, Aubrey, he shot your brother. His best friend. And,'' he added when Aubrey said nothing, ''Cory Silvan drives a green Explorer. We can't find any evidence that the white Firebird even exists.''

Chapter Thirteen

Lyle was clearly trying to get Aubrey to say something that would implicate Beau. He wheedled, he cajoled and he bullied, but Aubrey wouldn't oblige him.

"He didn't do anything wrong," she said with finality. "If you want to continue this conversation, you'll have to haul me into the station. Now, if you don't mind, I'm going to go find Sara."

She swept out of the library, hoping she'd sounded completely positive.

Because she wasn't.

Oh, not that Beau would kill someone in cold blood for money. But what if he and Rex had caught up with Cory? They could have taken the money, and what recourse did Cory have? He couldn't exactly go to the authorities and make a complaint. "Hey, these two bounty hunters stole my ransom money." They could have given him a portion, enough to shut him up, enough that he could make a new start someplace. And they could have provided the white Firebird story as a bogus tip, to give Cory more time to get away. Because if Cory were to be apprehended, a couple of bounty hunters would have their butts in a sling.

Aubrey didn't like it that her mind had come up

with this scenario. But what if Beau felt like he'd earned it? He'd risked his life on this case. He'd saved Aubrey's life, more than once.

She found Sara sitting in Wayne's lap. She'd never seen Wayne looking so besotted. Her uncle, who had always been a bit stern when she was a child, was babbling at his granddaughter like an idiot. The sight made her smile—perhaps for the first time that day.

The doorbell rang, and Aubrey didn't think much of it at first. People had been coming and going for hours. Wayne had left the front gates open, figuring it was safe with a bazillion cops around. But now most of the cops were gone. Still, it seemed unlikely that Cory remained a threat. Now that he'd gotten what he wanted, he would be long gone. Beronica went to see who it was.

Moments later she returned with Charlie Soffit at her side. A charged silence fell on the living room, but it was quickly broken by David's angry outburst.

"Just what the hell do you think you're doing here?" David started to move toward the other man, but Aubrey grabbed his sleeve and stopped him. Charlie's gaze had fixed on his daughter, and the emotions reflected there just about broke her heart—regret, love, grief, and a profound hunger.

"Easy," she said. "His daughter's just been found alive. Give him a break."

"Aubrey, he threatened to kill you," David reminded her.

"He was drunk and overwrought," she said. "He's calm and sober now. Let's let him see his daughter."

"Some father," David murmured.

Charlie spared a look to Aubrey. "Thanks. I know you don't owe me nothing. But I never had a choice with Sara, you know. Patti just took her away. I signed them papers because she said if I did, she'd let me visit sometimes.''

He stepped a bit closer to the baby. ''My God, she's beautiful. She looks like her mama, don't she?'' He leaned down even closer. ''Gonna be a heartbreaker. Like Patti.'' His eyes glistened with tears.

Wayne's face had gone stiff with disapproval, but he didn't object. Then Sara reached toward her father as if she wanted him to pick her up.

Charlie looked to Aubrey, since she appeared to be the only ally he had. ''Could I? Just for a minute?''

The thought of giving Charlie even this fleeting contact with Sara made Aubrey uneasy. But so much of her negative image of the man had come from Patti, and she now knew that Patti had been lying about that, along with a lot of other things.

Aubrey pushed a chair toward Charlie and invited him to sit. Then she picked Sara up from Wayne's lap and eased her gently into Charlie's. At least if he was sitting down, he couldn't do anything crazy, like run out the door with the baby.

But Charlie didn't seem interested in anything but his daughter. He held Sara like a fragile piece of china, running one index finger gently over her little mouth, her nose, her downy gold hair and her perfect, tiny hands.

When Sara grabbed his finger and held on, he looked like he'd just won the Texas Lotto. Everyone else was quiet, and Aubrey hoped they were as moved by the sight as she was.

Craig had told her Charlie had no criminal record before his arrest two days ago. He might be poor and uneducated, but if those were the worst of his crimes, it hardly seemed fair to deny him access to his daughter. Much as she didn't like the idea, Aubrey decided, as she watched Charlie watch Sara with rapt adoration, that she would investigate the possibility of letting Charlie have visitation—maybe after he'd taken a parenting course.

The phone rang. Since Beronica made no move to answer it, Aubrey slipped away from the group in the living room and answered the extension in the hallway.

It was Lyle Palmer. "Aubrey. I'm glad it's you. Listen, I want to apologize for my earlier behavior. I guess I was letting my distrust of Maddox rule my common sense."

"Has something happened?"

"Twenty minutes ago we arrested Cory Silvan. He was in his Explorer, not the white Firebird, but he did have the briefcase. Unfortunately, he had only a small portion of the ransom. He insists that's all there is, but we think he stashed the rest someplace because he knew he might get caught."

Aubrey felt a tremendous sense of relief. Her nightmare was well and truly over. But then she realized that the fact Cory only had a portion of the money— and no white Firebird—coincided a little too neatly with her theory about Beau.

She brushed that aside, because Lyle was giving her more information. "Cory has a bite mark on his right forearm, almost definitely human. And he was carrying a gun of the same caliber used by the sniper who shot at you. Of course, we'll have to do some lab tests, but my gut feeling is that he's our man."

"Thank God. Maybe I can actually sleep tonight. Lyle, thank you. I know we haven't always gotten along, but I do appreciate the work you put in on this case." Even if he wasn't the brightest bulb in the investigative world.

"You're welcome. Thanks for your part, too. How's Sara?"

"She's great." Aubrey decided not to mention Charlie Soffit's visit. "Lyle, you'll check into the possibility that Cory murdered Patti, won't you? She would never have willingly given Sara to that monster, so there must have been some foul play involved."

"I'll handle Cory's interrogation personally."

That did not fill Aubrey with confidence.

She returned to the living room and reported the good news. Everyone seemed overjoyed—except David, who looked decidedly troubled.

"What's wrong?" she asked him privately a few minutes later. Charlie had left, and Beronica had returned to the kitchen to resume cleanup. Only Wayne, David, Aubrey and a sleeping Sara remained in the living room.

"Cory said he'd kill me," David said, his voice breaking. "He said if I sent the cops after him, he'd track me down and shoot me like a rabid dog in the street. And if he couldn't do it personally, he had friends who could."

"That was just talk to scare you," Aubrey said, though she could certainly understand why her cousin was unnerved. "He's not the Godfather, he's a two-bit drug dealer. He's behind bars and likely to remain there for some time, particularly if you report the death threat."

"Still…" David laughed nervously. "Now I know how you felt the last few days."

"It's not much fun," she agreed, giving his arm an

affectionate squeeze. "But I really don't think you have to worry. In fact…" She looked at her watch. It was almost eleven o'clock. "I was thinking I might take Sara home now. Lyle assured me I would be safe."

"You know, I've been thinking about that," David said. "About Patti naming you as Sara's guardian."

"What?" Aubrey was suddenly alert to a new danger. A few days ago, David had agreed Aubrey was the logical one to raise Sara. But that was before they'd known Patti was actually dead. And now it seemed his feelings weren't so clear-cut.

"I'm Sara's closest living relative. Plus, I have resources you don't—money, connections. If I were to adopt Sara, she wouldn't want for anything. She could attend the best private schools, travel the world, land the best job or the wealthiest husband, whatever she wants. Think about it. You're an assistant college professor who lives in a run-down frame house in a questionable neighborhood."

Aubrey could not believe what she was hearing. She looked to Wayne—surely he would jump in and disagree with David. But to her horror, he was nodding. "You must agree, Aubrey, that he has a point."

"But Patti wanted *me* to raise Sara."

"And we all know how sound Patti's judgment was," David said. "I'm not sure the courts would take her wishes too seriously. She gave her baby to a drug dealer, after all."

"She did not—I don't believe this."

"I only want what's best for Sara," David insisted.

"Oh, right. When did you suddenly become so avuncular? Where were you when Patti was pregnant and needed help? You turned her away. You refused her money. You didn't go to the hospital when Sara was born, even though I notified you."

"Patti wouldn't have welcomed our presence," Wayne said.

"You weren't around for the 2:00 a.m. feedings and the ear infection that sent us to the hospital," Aubrey continued relentlessly. "You saw her all of, what, twice since she was born?"

"Aubrey, you have to understand," Wayne said, his tone condescending. "Patti made it very difficult for either of us to play a role in Sara's life. But now that she's gone—and now that I've seen Sara, spent time with her—I realize we made a mistake in not trying harder to heal the breach. I would like to spend what little time I have left with my only granddaughter. Is that so hard to understand?"

Aubrey got the distinct impression that Wayne and David had discussed this earlier. "Are you saying you won't let me take her home?"

"This is her home now," David said. "I won't have her living in that house, vulnerable to unsavory influences. Charlie Soffit, for God's sake. Would you actually let that man have a role in my niece's life? And Beau Maddox. A low-life bounty hunter. He shot your own brother, for chrissakes. I'm not at all sure your new friends would be positive influences on Sara's life."

"Oh, and your newfound interest in Sara wouldn't have anything to do with the fact that she'll someday be a multimillionaire, would it?" Aubrey had taken off the gloves. If David was going to fight dirty, so was she.

"I don't need money," David said.

"Oh, don't you? Then just exactly what was it I

heard the partners talking about earlier, at the funeral?'' Now she realized she'd piqued Wayne's attention, and she remembered he didn't know anything about his partners' suspicions. Maybe it wasn't her place to tell him. But it was a little late to turn back now.

''What the hell are you talking about?'' David demanded.

''Jim Thomason. And the guy with the toupee—''

''Mark Jeeter,'' Wayne supplied impatiently. ''What did they say?''

''I don't know the specifics,'' Aubrey said. ''But it was clear they believe David is guilty of some financial misdeed. And Beau told me the police did some investigating—as they investigated everyone in the family,'' she hastened to add. ''It's routine. But they found something more than routine debt when they investigated you, David. I believe the word they used was *obscene.*''

She let the accusation rest on the air for a few seconds. Maybe she'd gone too far. She had, after all, eavesdropped on a private conversation. And the police information was secondhand.

Wayne suddenly looked unutterably weary. ''We're all exhausted,'' he said. ''And we're probably saying things we don't mean. This whole situation will look much brighter in the morning. I suggest we all get some sleep.''

''I'm not leaving without Sara,'' Aubrey said mulishly.

''Of course not, my dear. You're welcome to stay here for as long as you like. For God's sake, we're a family. Maybe we should try acting like one.''

Aubrey put Sara to bed on a pallet in her room. Neither of the men objected to that, of course. Neither of them wanted to change diapers. If Sara lived here permanently, Wayne would no doubt immediately hire a nanny.

Aubrey could take him at his word and live here, too. But she thought Sara would be much better off in her unassuming little house, raised as normally as possible. All that privilege and money hadn't done Patti a world of good. Or David, for that matter, she thought, her earlier surge of affection for him having disintegrated.

Tired as she was, Aubrey couldn't sleep. Sara, possibly picking up on her restlessness, woke up fussy at about midnight. Aubrey got her up, gave her a bottle of water, then walked with her. She walked the halls upstairs, then from room to room downstairs, and finally out the front door. The idea crossed her mind that she could jump in her car and drive off, but she dismissed it. Such impulsive behavior would only hurt her chances later of getting custody of Sara.

The night was beautiful—clear, a little cooler than it had been recently, with just a hint of breeze. Aubrey paced the huge front porch, then the driveway, then found a seat on the bench by the fountain, where she'd sat talking with Beau after the gas leak.

Her mind raced with turmoil. Would David and Wayne really take Sara away from her? She was as bonded to this child as Sara's own mother had been. With Aubrey's love and guidance, she was sure Sara could overcome her questionable birth parentage. Without it, who knew?

And that wasn't all that troubled Aubrey. Her thoughts returned again and again to Beau. She tried to tell herself that of course he didn't take any money. If he had, Cory would have ratted him out immediately. Right? Unless Lyle hadn't told her that part. Maybe he considered her a suspect, in possible collusion with Beau, and his nicey-nicey act was part of some plot to get her to spill her guts.

She would feel a lot better if she could simply see Beau, talk to him. But he'd stayed away, a fact that didn't bode well for his innocence—or for any future relationship they might have. It scared her to admit she would even consider a relationship. But it scared her more to think of a future without Beau, forever and ever without Beau.

Maybe she should tell him how she felt. Or she could talk to Lori Bettencourt, who might have some insight on how to handle the situation. Though she'd only spent a few minutes with the neophyte bounty hunter, Aubrey had felt an instant connection with her, as if the two of them could become friends.

But even as she considered revealing her newly discovered love, something inside her clamped down. She'd spent so many years hiding her feelings or masking them with animosity. The idea of leaving herself so vulnerable made her insides freeze up with fear. If he rejected her now, it would be so, so much worse. They'd connected on some intimate level that went beyond physical lovemaking, wonderful though that had been. The connection was real. But she had no idea whether it was anything Beau wanted to sustain. After all, he'd made it almost to thirty with no serious relationship.

But maybe love, real love, required some risk.

Sara was quiet now, asleep. The bottle and the walking had done the trick. Aubrey stood and headed up the steps to the front porch. As she reached for the door, a hand settled lightly on her shoulder.

She whirled around, instinctively covering the baby with both arms, a scream in her throat. Then she saw it was Beau.

"Damn it, Beau. Can't you ever approach like a normal person?"

BEAU RECOILED slightly. This wasn't the reception he'd been hoping for. God, she looked pretty in the soft light of the front porch, her hair loose and tousled from sleep, her nightshirt failing to disguise the intriguing shape of her breasts.

"The gates are open," Aubrey continued. "You could have just driven down the driveway. What did you do, scale the fence instead?"

"I wasn't sure I was welcome."

"I'm not sure you are, either," she said cautiously. "Where have you been? Why the disappearing act?"

"Rex got a call just when I caught up with him. He needed help with a takedown. He got hurt and needed to go to the hospital—just some stitches, nothing serious," he added when her look changed to one of concern. "But I ended up processing our bail-jumper. And that can take hours." It had taken a few more hours to work up the courage to return to the Clarendon mansion. Now that his professional services were no longer needed, he didn't have a clue where he stood with Aubrey.

"Well, your absence was noted," she said, a little more friendly now. "Lyle was sure you'd murdered Cory in the woods, nabbed the million dollars, and that you were en route to Venezuela."

"Ah, hell, that just figures."

She opened the door. "Come on inside," she said, sounding almost resigned. "Everyone else is in bed. I'll get us something to drink. Any particular reason you're showing up now?"

"Isn't it enough that I wanted to see you? And the kid? I just got a glimpse of her earlier. She's okay, isn't she?" As he followed Aubrey toward the kitchen, he studied the sleeping baby, whom Aubrey had propped on her shoulder. She looked fine, but Beau knew nothing about babies. He'd almost never been this close to such a small one.

"She's fine." Aubrey went to the huge, stainless-steel fridge and opened it, studying the contents. Then she turned back to Beau. "Would you like to hold her while I get our drinks?"

"Who, me?"

"Come on, it won't kill you." She held the sleeping child out to him. Reluctantly he took Sara, holding her at arm's length for a few seconds, until he realized that wasn't going to work. The baby was waking up, and she didn't look happy about the change of sleeping arrangements. Her face crumpled and she let out a sob.

Tamping down panic, Beau cradled her against his chest, trying to mimic the way Aubrey had held her, but she didn't stop fussing.

"Jiggle her a little bit," Aubrey suggested. He got the distinct impression she was enjoying this, that she'd done it to make him uncomfortable.

He did as ordered, jiggling and rocking back and forth. Miraculously, the baby quieted. She relaxed and snuggled up against him. She felt kind of like a puppy, he realized, and he liked puppies, although he'd never admit that aloud. He continued to rock her, pacing around the huge kitchen. Sara's eyes drooped, and soon she was asleep again.

Grinning, Aubrey poured out two huge glasses of cold milk and set them on the table. "I'll take her back if you want," she said, holding out her hands, no doubt figuring he'd jump at the chance to unload his burden.

"Not yet. I'm just getting the hang of this." Beau felt this strange, alien creature inside himself—a creature that wanted to hold on to the baby. It felt...*nice,* holding a child, keeping it safe, making it feel secure. Was this why women wanted babies, why their biological clocks ticked? He'd never imagined he would have children, but he'd never seen the appeal before. Of course, the crying, spitting up and dirty diapers were a pretty high price to pay for a few moments of maternal bliss—or paternal, in his case.

After a few more moments he handed the baby back to Aubrey, hoping she didn't notice his reluctance. If she did, she said nothing. She settled down in a chair at the kitchen table and drank her milk. Beau did the same.

"She's exhausted from the ordeal, of course, but a little too wound up to sleep normally. And she's been eating like crazy. God knows what that cretin was feeding her. Thank God he's finally behind bars."

That stopped Beau cold. "Cory?"

"You didn't hear? The cops caught up with him a few hours ago. He was dumb enough to return to his apartment. He had a bite mark on his arm and the same kind of gun that our sniper had. Lyle seems to think they can make quite a case against him—and possibly tie him to Patti's death, too."

"That's good news."

"They didn't find him in a white Firebird, though." She paused, as if waiting for a reaction from him. When he said nothing else, she continued. "And he only had a small portion of the money with him."

Suddenly, with a bolt of clarity, Beau saw what was going on here. He set down his half-full milk glass, so hard he sloshed a bit of the liquid over the side. "You think I took it."

"No, of course not!" she said hotly. "It's just an oddity that needs to be explained."

"You think I caught Cory, took the money, left him just enough that he could start over someplace and made up some story about a white Firebird." He could not believe this.

Aubrey's mouth moved, but no words came out. Sara, perhaps sensing the tension, stirred and fretted.

"Does that story sound familiar?" he prodded her.

Finally she managed to find her voice. "Lyle thinks—"

"I don't care what Lyle thinks. I care what Aubrey thinks."

"Okay. Okay, it did cross my mind. But maybe I have a devious mind. And if you tell me it's not true, that Cory got away clean, I'll believe you."

"I told you once exactly what happened," he said, barely holding in his temper. It was a good thing she had a baby in her arms, or he'd have gotten right in her face, just to make sure he was perfectly clear. "How many times do I have to tell you? I don't know how many times I told you your brother pointed a gun at me, but it didn't matter. You didn't believe me then and you won't believe me now."

"But I want to believe you now."

He raked his hands through his hair. This was so

pointless. "You know why it took me so long to come back here tonight? Because I had to work my courage up. I wanted to find out if we had a chance, even a small chance, of making a go of it. Guess I would have done better to go out and get drunk. Obviously we've got nothing if you think I'm the kind of guy who would—"

He turned and stalked out of the kitchen.

"Beau, wait. This came out all wrong," she said, trotting behind him to keep up. "God, I'm not even sure I'd blame you if you did take the money. You certainly earned it."

He couldn't let that pass. He whirled around, almost running into her. "I don't want your forgiveness for sins I didn't commit. I want you to look me in the eye and know in your heart that I am not the kind of man who would shoot my best friend or let a murderous, kidnapping drug dealer go free for a few bucks. But when you look me in the eye, I see suspicion. And I can't live with that, even if you can."

He turned again and completed his escape.

Chapter Fourteen

"Ninety-eight, ninety-nine, one hundred." Beau collapsed to the floor. He hadn't done *that* in a while— a hundred push-ups. His arms burned, and his every pore rained sweat.

"Nice show," Lori said from her desk, where she was working on some skip-traces at her computer. "What demons are chasing you?"

"I haven't the slightest idea..." He stopped to gulp some water from a bottle. "...what you're talking about."

"Just that you only come in here and work out like a maniac when something's bothering you. Damn, I hate this guy," she muttered at the computer. "He's got enough identities to start his own football team."

Well, hell. Lori was pretty perceptive, but Beau already knew that. She was going to be a helluva bounty hunter when she got trained up a bit.

"Does it have to do with the Clarendon baby?" she asked. "Duh, of course," she added before he could answer, thumping herself in the head with the heel of her hand. "What have you been working on nonstop for the last few days?"

"That's it, all right," he agreed. "It ticks me off I

didn't get the reward." He'd tried to tell himself a thousand times over the past twenty-four hours that that's what had him tied up in knots. He should have gone after Cory. He'd suspected the drug dealer was involved somehow with Patti's death and Sara's disappearance. But he couldn't convince himself to stray too far or for too long from Aubrey. And that had probably cost him the reward.

"A million dollars would have been nice," Lori agreed blandly. "But that's not what's bugging you. I know what motivates you. And it's not money."

"How can you say that?" he asked, messing with the weights on the home gym so he could do some leg extensions. "Why do you think I became a bounty hunter?"

"Ace became a bounty hunter for the money," she said. "You did it so you could right wrongs. Take down nasty criminals. Find lost children before any harm comes to them."

"You make me sound like some kind of saint. Honey, I'm far from that."

"Not a saint," Lori agreed. She abandoned her computer search and walked over to watch him sweat. Or so she could look him in the eye. "It's Aubrey Schuyler, isn't it?"

"What? No, of course not." He knew he'd denied it a little too quickly.

"There's some kind of spark between you two. Come on, you can tell me. What happened while you were protecting her body? Did you do a little more than protect it?"

Damn, but she had a way of prying the truth out of a person. He'd take Lori with him next time he needed to interrogate someone. He didn't answer her, but his silence told her what she wanted to know.

"Want some advice?" she asked brightly.

"No."

"I'll give it to you anyway. She's as hot on you as you are on her. A woman can tell these things about other women."

"I shot her brother. She's not going to get over that."

"She could."

Beau just shook his head. "Drop it, okay?"

Lori shrugged as Beau began his next set. "Okay. Oh, your friend Craig called. Something about wanting your input on the evidence against Cory Silvan."

"Like I'm an expert on the guy?" But Craig usually didn't make frivolous requests. Beau made a mental note to call when he was done with his workout— which might be next week, since all this straining and sweating hadn't managed to purge his convoluted feelings for Aubrey from his system.

"So, how come we've never met this friend?" Lori asked.

"Craig? He's a cop, that's why. He can't hang out with bounty hunters. Not good for his reputation."

"He sounds cute over the phone."

"How can anyone 'sound cute'?"

"So, is he?"

Beau rolled his eyes. "He's a doll. A real dreamboat."

"I'm serious."

"Lori, we've been over this. Guys don't think other guys are cute. But Craig Cartwright doesn't lack for female companionship, if that's what you mean. Why, you looking for some action?"

"Not me. I've given up on men. Once they find out what I do for a living they're either intimidated as hell, in which case, who needs 'em, or they want me to quit immediately and get a job as a secretary because they can't stand worrying about me. But I have single friends."

"Hmph, you've never introduced them to me."

"I wouldn't do that to my friends."

"Ouch, Lori. Kick a man when he's down."

But she was giggling. "Call Craig back. And then let me talk to him."

"You're a piece of work." But he dried the sweat off his face and hands, then sat down at one of the empty desks and dialed Craig's cell number.

"I'm not sure I can help," Beau said as soon as he had Craig on the line.

"I just need your gut instinct. What do you think Cory might have done with the rest of the ransom money?"

"Hell, I don't know. He could have left it with a friend. He could have buried it. Or maybe it's in the white Firebird. I understand Lyle thinks I fabricated that car."

"Not anymore. It was reported stolen this morning. We found it abandoned in a field, wiped clean. And no money in it."

"Well, hallelujah."

"It just seems a little strange, that's all. Cory claims there was never a million dollars in the briefcase, that it was only thirteen thousand, but he was in a hurry and didn't check."

"Wait a minute, Craig. He *did* check. Before he turned over the baby, David opened the briefcase for him to verify that the money was there."

"Did he count it?"

"No. But how could he mistake thirteen thousand dollars for a million? He's a drug dealer, not some clueless kid."

They were both silent for a few moments.

"Thirteen thousand?" Beau asked, just to be sure.

"Yeah."

"Ah, hell. That's exactly how much Patti owed Cory. That's why he was threatening her, why he probably killed her. For thirteen thousand dollars. How pathetic."

Another silence.

"Cory knew," Beau finally said. "He knew exactly how much money David was giving him. Cory wanted to collect that million-dollar reward, but he couldn't, not without implicating himself in Patti's murder."

"So he worked some kind of deal with David Clarendon?"

"Exactly." Beau was getting excited as the implications mushroomed inside his head. "David needed money. He apparently embezzled from the law firm, or was involved in some sort of financial malfeasance."

"So he got cash for the reward money from the bank," Craig said, obviously on the same page as Beau, "gave a small portion to Cory—"

"—and paid back the money he stole from the firm, probably managing to keep a nice chunk for his other debts. That little scumbag!"

"Wait a minute. Before we get carried away…"

"What? It's the perfect answer to the mystery."

"Why would Cory settle for so little? There was no reason for him to work a deal with David for a paltry thirteen thousand. He could have found someone unconnected with the case who could claim they'd found Sara in a trash can, collect the million-dollar reward, and split it with him.''

"Unless…" Beau's mind worked furiously. "Unless David was calling the shots.''

"He had something on Cory, some leverage," Craig added.

Beau snapped his fingers. "He knew Cory killed Patti. May have even put him up to it.''

"Why would he want to kill his sister?''

"To get control of Sara's trust fund. He was sore because the old man had cut him out of the will.''

"But didn't you tell me Aubrey was named Sara's trustee?''

Aubrey. Oh, hell. Oh, *hell*. "I have to go get Aubrey out of there," he said urgently. "She could still be in danger. She's the only person left standing in the way of David getting control of the family fortune. David was involved in one murder. He might not stop there.''

"I'll get a team up to speed and be right behind you. Don't do anything crazy. Just go in easy, make sure she's safe." Craig apparently knew Beau well enough not to order him to wait.

Beau hung up the phone, grabbed his car keys from the desk where he'd left them, and walked out of First Strike.

AUBREY HAD what she could only call a stress hangover the next day. Fortunately, Sara had slept through the night, and so had Aubrey—the deepest, most profound sleep she'd had in days. But she hadn't awakened feeling refreshed. She'd felt leaden, like she'd swallowed a jar full of fishing weights, or her brain had magically turned into a barbell overnight.

Sluggish and puffy, she took a warm shower, then turned on the cold water and tried to snap herself out of it. Sara was safe! She should be dancing with joy.

But she wasn't. She'd realized she was in love with Beau, only to drive him away with her suspicions—totally unfounded, she learned at breakfast, because the white Firebird had been discovered. She also had to contend with the unexpected hostility from David, and the very real possibility that her cousin would take Sara away from her.

It was hard to feel cheerful under those circumstances.

At least Sara woke up cheerful. She babbled and cooed all through breakfast, banging a wooden spoon on the old high chair Beronica had loaned them, and she ate her mushed-up eggs like a linebacker.

Wayne wasn't at the breakfast table with them. Yesterday had taken its toll on him, and he'd told Beronica he wasn't feeling well enough to come downstairs. Mary arrived while they were eating.

David left for the office after breakfast. Of course, he'd probably neglected a lot of work over the past few days, but Aubrey felt he could have at least checked on his father before cutting out. Then she reminded herself to go easy on David. Just because she disagreed with him over Sara's custody didn't mean she should assign nefarious motivations to his every action. He'd been caring for Wayne for months, now, a responsibility that had its own stresses and strains.

Aubrey helped Beronica clean up the kitchen. She wasn't used to having servants wait on her, and it bothered her. She didn't really want Sara to grow up that way, either. She wanted the child to learn to take care of herself—cook, clean, do laundry. Otherwise she'd end up as clueless as Patti when she grew up.

The rest of the house was still a wreck. Aubrey knew Beronica was supposed to leave at noon today for her regular day-and-a-half off, and she probably wouldn't want to leave the house less than tidy. So Aubrey pitched in there, too, though Beronica told her it wasn't necessary.

There were dirty glasses, cocktail plates, forks and napkins all over the downstairs, littering every surface. Aubrey started by picking those up and taking them to the kitchen.

Next she went around collecting literally dozens of sterling coasters. "Where do these go?" she asked Beronica.

"There." Beronica pointed to a side table in the living room. Aubrey opened the drawer and found that same baby toy, the green plastic key chain, peeking out.

"Oh, Beronica, here. I found this under the sofa. It's Carlos's, yes?"

Beronica stared at the toy a few moments, a puzzled look on her face. "No, I never saw it. Oh, maybe it belong to Sara?"

"No, it's been here a few days."

Beronica nodded. "*Sí*, she maybe forget it when she visit another time."

"But she never—" Aubrey stopped herself. Surely this was just a case of miscommunication because of the language barrier. "Did you see Sara here another time?"

Beronica nodded. "She come with her mama. Last Monday, *yo creo*. I see picture of Patti on the television."

"Patti and Sara came here? Last Monday?" Aubrey asked again, just to be sure. That was the day Patti had died and Sara had disappeared.

"*Si*. Señor David talk to her, long time, I think."

Aubrey's heart pounded. Why had David lied about that? And what else had he lied about? "Beronica, this is *muy importante*. Did David leave the house that day? After Patti's visit?" Aubrey was ashamed at what she was thinking. David might be dishonest, but surely he couldn't be involved in murdering his own sister.

Beronica took a moment to think. Then she shook her head decisively. "No. He stay with his papa, and he work in *la oficina*." She pointed upstairs, toward the room David had converted to a home office.

Aubrey took a deep breath and allowed herself a small sigh of relief. Still, why had he lied? Had he been afraid the police would suspect—but no, he'd lied long before anyone knew Patti was dead.

Unless he'd known.

A chill wiggled up her spine.

Beronica checked her watch, then returned to polishing the furniture with renewed vigor, apparently assuming the discussion was over.

Had the police never questioned Beronica? No one in the family had been considered a serious suspect, but in any investigation of foul play, the family had to be ruled out. Any competent detective would have at least talked briefly with the servants. But *competent* was the operative word here. She already knew Lyle was lazy and not that bright.

Aubrey was torn about what to do with this new information. She knew what she wanted to do. She wanted to call Beau. He would understand the significance. He would know what to do. But she couldn't call him now, not after the way they'd parted last night. He probably never wanted to talk to her again.

Shortly before noon, Beronica left for her day off. Aubrey played with Sara, but her mind churned with scenarios. Maybe she should simply confront David with the lie. That might be the best option. He would probably have a perfectly convincing explanation for why he'd lied, though she didn't know what that could be.

Mary came downstairs looking solemn. "Is David here?" she asked.

"No, he went to the office. Is anything wrong?"

"Your uncle's not doing well. He's in a lot of pain. I'm afraid this ordeal with his daughter and grand-daughter has sapped what little strength he had left. His vital signs are erratic."

"Can you give him something for the pain?" Aubrey asked, alarmed.

"Yes, but he doesn't want me to give him any morphine. It knocks him out, and he's afraid he won't wake up again. Frankly, he might be right. I don't want to upset anyone unnecessarily, but I've been doing this a long time. Typically a patient rallies briefly, then there's a fast downhill slide."

"And yesterday was his rally." Damn. This really wasn't fair. Wayne was just getting to know his grand-daughter. It was too soon. "I'll call David."

David was "unavailable," but she left a message that he needed to come home right away. Then she took Sara upstairs to see Wayne.

He looked worse than ever. His complexion was gray, his eyes sunken, his hands positively skeletal. She pasted on a smile. "Mary says you're not feeling so hot today."

His eyes fluttered open, and he managed a weak smile of his own. "That's a bit of an understatement." His voice was weak and thready, his breath rapid and shallow. He looked at Mary, who had followed Aubrey back to the sickroom. "Help me sit up."

Mary expertly lifted Wayne until he was almost sitting up. She put an extra pillow behind his back. "Would you like me to leave you all alone for a while? Can I get you anything?"

"You don't happen to have one of those KitKat bars handy, do you? I have a craving."

She smiled. "If that's what you want, I'll run to the store and get one." She looked to Aubrey. "Is that okay?"

"Of course."

Wayne smiled weakly. "You're a good nurse, Mary."

When they were alone, Aubrey set Sara in Wayne's lap. She knew that was what he wanted.

"I was holding on for her," he said, stroking Sara's silky blond hair. "Now that she's safe, I'm not needed here."

"Don't say that. Of course you're needed. We wouldn't know what to do if…"

"Well, you'd better figure it out. I won't make it another twenty-four hours."

Aubrey wanted to argue, but Wayne had a knowing look in his eye. He wasn't just being melodramatic.

"I wanted to say goodbye. And to apologize, for letting my feud with Patti get the better of me. I shouldn't have been so proud. I should have tried— ah, but I guess everyone has regrets."

"Everyone," she agreed, including herself in that pool.

"David is going to fight you for Sara's custody," he continued. He seemed to be struggling through every sentence, and he had to pause and breathe after each one. "Hire Ron Beasley to represent you. He's the best family law attorney I know."

"You want me to win? What you said last night—"

"I thought about that last night. Hell, I didn't do much else but think. Couldn't sleep. I love you both, but you're practically Sara's mother already. Anyway, David only wants Sara so he can get hold of my money." At Aubrey's surprised expression, he added, "I talked to Jim. David's been embezzling. No question."

"But you said David didn't care about money."

"I said he had a strange attitude about money. He always acted as if there were an endless supply of it, which made him *appear* unconcerned. But he's already burned his way through the two million dollars his grandfather left him, and possibly a good chunk of the firm's assets as well."

"Oh, my God. What are we going to do?"

"Not we, you. I don't have the strength to confront him. That's your job."

The doorbell rang. Aubrey stood, relieved to pause this conversation. It was a lot to absorb. "I should get that. Beronica's not here." She didn't want to fight David. She didn't want any more evidence that he was desperate about money. Because that meant she had to confront the possibility he'd been involved in Patti's death—or that he knew something about the missing ransom money, she thought suddenly. "I'll be right back."

The doorbell chimed three more times before she got downstairs. Someone was awfully impatient. Still a little jumpy from the last few days, she peeked through the peephole. And there was Beau, standing on the porch.

She'd never been so happy to see him.

She swung the door open. "I'm so glad you're here."

"I'm glad to see you're okay," he said in a hushed voice. "Is David here?"

"No, he's at work. What's going on?"

"I think you and Sara may be in danger here. Wayne, too."

"Wayne's dying," she said bluntly. "The hospice nurse says he only has a few hours."

"I'm sorry," Beau said as he stepped inside, the sentiment obviously genuine. "But he might not be the only one. I believe David was involved in Sara's disappearance. He and Cory were in cahoots, somehow. Cory murdered Patti and took Sara. Then he and David worked some kind of deal. I'm sorry," Beau said again. "I know you probably don't believe me. I know how hard it is for you to believe that someone you love, someone you're related to, could do something so awful. But you have to believe me. You're in danger."

"You have no idea how happy I am to hear you say that."

"What?" Clearly he'd been prepared for a different response from her.

"David has been lying. Patti and Sara were here the day she died. Beronica saw them here, but no one thought to question her. Those toy keys *do* belong to Sara. And Wayne just told me some things about David and his…lust for money. I don't want to believe it, but…"

"David only gave Cory thirteen thousand dollars."

"The exact amount Patti owed Cory."

"David had leverage. Because he knew Cory murdered Patti."

"And he kept the rest of the million dollars. That's probably what he's doing today—replacing the money he stole from the law firm. And he must be the one who shot at me. His fingerprints wouldn't be on the AFIS computer."

They heard a noise, and both of them turned to see what it was. David was lounging in the doorway that led from the foyer to the kitchen. And he held a gun pointed at them. Not the little .22 she'd seen him use at other times, but a big semi-automatic.

"Very clever, cousin," he said with a smug smile. "You're absolutely right."

Chapter Fifteen

Show no fear. Beau repeated that phrase like a mantra, because he knew David Clarendon wanted to see them cower. He knew this because he knew David. He remembered the child with the cruel streak who put a lot of his energy into teasing pets and neighborhood kids and his younger sister.

Hell, he should have seen this coming. He should have known David was involved. The police dismissed him as a suspect so easily. But when a suspicious death occurred in any family with money, chances were a family member was involved.

"David, put that gun away!" Aubrey blustered, using her schoolteacher voice.

But he made no move to lower the gun. "You two have put me in a very awkward position. I didn't kill anyone. That stupid drug dealer was supposed to scare Patti, rough her up a bit. Get her arrested. Get her in trouble with the child-welfare people."

"So you could take Sara away from her," Aubrey concluded.

"So I could get what's rightfully mine!" David's face twisted with emotion. "I'm the one who stuck by Dad's side. I got the good grades, I followed in his footsteps. I never set one foot out of line, never got in trouble. I supported him one hundred percent at the firm. I sat second chair on the high-profile cases, doing all the work while he got all the glory.''

Just keep talking, Beau thought, one by one going through his options, though he didn't have many. His own gun was at the small of his back. He started inching his hand toward it, knowing any sudden move he made could get Aubrey killed.

''When Dad got sick, I was the one who listened to him cry like a baby. I sat with him through—'' Suddenly David's gaze zeroed in on Beau. ''You reach for that gun and you'll be sorry! Put your hands on top of your head. Now!''

Beau complied, silently cursing. If David had any expertise with guns, he would take Beau's gun away. But he wasn't accustomed to holding a weapon or shooting it. He looked clumsy with it. Which only made him more dangerous.

''I sat with Dad through chemo,'' David continued, addressing his comments to Aubrey. ''I held his head when he couldn't keep his food down.''

''And you did this for love?'' Aubrey asked skeptically. ''Or for profit?''

''I loved my father,'' David said, as if he thought he should get a medal. ''Until he stabbed me in the back.''

''By cutting you out of the will.''

''There was no reason for it! What did I do? I didn't run away from home or get addicted to drugs or litter the town with bastard children.''

''No, you just embezzled from the firm. And ordered your sister's death.''

''I didn't do that!'' David insisted. ''Killing Patti

and taking Sara was all Cory's idea. He was the one who shot at you, too. He said you made him nervous. He went completely over the edge.''

"But you made it work in your favor, didn't you," Aubrey taunted.

"It all would have worked out fine if you hadn't gotten so damn nosy about my business. I would have been happy with almost a million in cash.''

"No, you wouldn't. You were already challenging me for Sara's custody. No amount of money would have satisfied you.''

Good girl, Beau thought as he tried a different tack, gradually putting distance between himself and Aubrey. The farther apart they stood, the harder it would be for David to keep an eye on both of them. And as he moved, inch by inch, away from Aubrey, he moved closer to David. He would rush David if he had to, chance the gunshot wound. David wouldn't have time to aim properly. If Beau was lucky, the shot would go wild.

"I think I know why Uncle Wayne changed his will," Aubrey said. "He just looked into your eyes and knew he'd been mistaken. *You* were the bad seed, not Patti.''

"So what now?" Beau asked, breaking his silence. He didn't want Aubrey to go too far and provoke her cousin to an anger he couldn't control.

David jumped and swung the gun toward Beau. "Hey. What do you think you're doing?"

"I'm coming over to take that gun away from you," Beau said, trying to inject as much confidence into his voice as he could. "You haven't killed anyone yet. Do you think you'll get away with it? How are you going to explain two people shot in the foyer of your father's house? For embezzling and extortion, you're good for maybe twenty or thirty years. Time off for good behavior, maybe out in ten or fifteen. If you murder someone, you'll get caught. I've already talked to the police about you. No matter what you set up— murder-suicide, or a story about Cory's friends exacting revenge—you'll be suspect number one. They'll find the gunpowder residue on your hands. You'll end up on death row.''

Beau's speech was not having the desired effect. Doubt was supposed to be flickering in David's eyes right about now. His gun hand was supposed to be wavering. Instead, he wore a chilling little smile.

As Beau continued to creep closer to David, David did some maneuvering of his own, toward the front door.

Beau considered telling him not to bother running. Craig was already on his way with a cadre of uniformed officers ready to move in and make the arrest. But he decided it would be better if David *did* think running was his best option. Certainly preferable to a double murder.

Close to the door now, David reached up and plucked the dead bolt key from its hook and gripped it in his free hand.

''I'm not quite as stupid as you think,'' he said with a wink as he let himself out. The door slammed, and the lock snicked into place.

And just like that, it was over.

Beau rushed to Aubrey and they flung themselves into each other's arms. She was trembling with the aftereffects of fear and relief.

''Oh, my God, Beau, I thought he was going to kill us.''

"I did, too. You did great, keeping him talking."

She laughed almost hysterically. "I don't even know what I was saying. I think I sounded like some character in a melodrama." She glanced nervously toward the door. "Do you think he's really gone?"

They both heard the start of a car engine—David's Porsche, from the roar of it.

"Sounds like it." Beau peeked out the peephole. He could see the red car sitting in the driveway, top down. David sat there, not moving, staring at the house. "Don't you dare change your mind, you bastard." Beau grabbed one of the delicate antique chairs that stood against the foyer wall and jammed it up under the double doorknobs. It might at least slow him down.

"We should call the police," Aubrey said.

"Craig's already on his way—he should be here by now."

"Let's call him anyway, tell him to hurry. After all this, I don't want David to get away."

"Okay." Beau kissed her on the forehead before heading into the living room. He wanted to tell her he loved her. He wanted to let her know how terrified he'd been when he realized she was in danger, and how devastated he would have been if he'd lost her. How protecting her and Sara was the only thing that kept him from running after David and chasing him down himself.

But this time, he was going to leave the police work to the cops. He wasn't going to end up shooting another of Aubrey's relatives, no matter what he'd done.

Aubrey followed him to the phone in the living room. He reached for it, then paused. Something was bothering him.

"Beau? I smell gas."

That's what it was. The front door. There wasn't a logical reason for David to take the time to lock the door behind himself. And he'd made a point of taking the key.

"He didn't have to shoot us," Beau said as the horror sank in. "He's gassing us. Probably overheard us, then turned on the gas before he confronted us. After the close call you had the other night, no one will suspect it's anything other than an accident. Is the shutoff outside?"

"Yes. Oh, Beau, we're locked in!"

He reached for the phone, but Aubrey grabbed his hand before he could lift the receiver. "No! Methane is very explosive. Pick up the phone or turn on a light, and the electrical connection could ignite the gas and blow up the whole house! We should open the windows. Slowly, though. The sudden influx of oxygen could cause an explosion, too."

They each ran to a living-room window, but opening them helped very little. The outside shutters were closed and latched, and the burglar bars insured they could not escape that way.

"It's no use," Aubrey said. "All the windows on the first two floors are barred and most of them shuttered. We need to get out of here. And—oh, my God, we have to get Uncle Wayne and Sara out!"

"The back door—"

"—has a double-keyed dead bolt, too, and you can bet David locked it." The smell of gas was very strong now, and Aubrey wavered a bit on her feet. "We have to go up. The mixture of gases they use in this area has a lot of propane in the mix, so it tends to sink. It'll be strongest down here." She was already heading for the stairs. "We'll get Sara and Uncle Wayne and go up to the servants' quarters on the third floor. Beronica's not there, but she has a private entrance and fire escape."

"Good," Beau said, starting to feel a little woozy himself as he followed Aubrey up the stairs. "Good thinking."

When they entered Wayne's room, he was sitting up in bed, but he looked as if he'd nodded off. Both he and the baby appeared to be asleep.

"Oh, God, no!" Aubrey cried. "They're both smaller and weaker than us. Maybe the gas—" But Sara woke up the moment Aubrey picked her up. "Oh, thank God, oh, baby, you're all right. Uncle Wayne! Wake up!"

The old man stirred groggily. "Hmm?" His bleary eyes appeared unfocused.

"Uncle Wayne, we have to get out of the house. It's filled with natural gas."

"Wha—gas?"

Aubrey yanked his covers back and attempted to pull him upright, but even in his emaciated condition, his dead weight was too much for her.

"I'll get him," Beau said. "Take the baby and go ahead. We'll be right behind you."

"But—"

"Go! Get Sara to safety."

Aubrey's eyes filled with tears. "Hurry." Then she turned and ran out the door with the crying baby.

Beau turned his attention to Wayne. "Come on, Wayne, we've got to get you out of here." He threw the old man's arms over his shoulder and attempted to grasp him in a fireman's carry.

"No, leave me be!" Wayne objected, fighting the maneuver.

"I won't do that."

"I'm dying anyway, you fool. Save Sara and Aubrey. Take care of them."

Beau ignored the old man's pleas and hoisted him up over his shoulder. "We can all make it. We just have to go up and out." He carried Wayne with little effort—the poor man wasn't much more than a bag of bones.

"Fool," Wayne muttered, but he ran out of fight.

Beau strode to the stairs and started up them, but Aubrey met him coming down. "The door to the upstairs apartment is locked!"

"I'll break it down."

"Solid wood," Wayne murmured. "Need an ax."

"You two wait here," Aubrey said. "Let me check the back staircase."

She handed Sara to Beau and took off like a bullet, but she returned less than a minute later. "It's locked, too. We'll have to…I don't know! I don't know how much longer we can last!"

"Wayne," Aubrey said as Beau set him gently down on the stairs, "are there any windows without bars on this floor?"

He shook his head. "No."

"Is there a crawl space?" Beau asked, wracking his brain for some other means of escape. "An air-conditioning duct, maybe?" He was grasping at straws, now, but he refused to accept defeat. If he was going out, he would go out fighting.

"The dumbwaiter," Aubrey said suddenly. "Sara and I can go up in it. Then we can open the door for you two. Come on."

"I'll wait here," Wayne said, almost collapsing against the stairs. "Air's…fresher…here."

"Take a few deep breaths," Beau told Aubrey. He followed his own directions, and they headed downstairs.

"I may not fit in the dumbwaiter," Aubrey said. "I'm sure I outgrew it a long time ago."

"You'll fit if I have to wedge you in with a crowbar."

The smell of gas was very strong now. Beau hoped he could hold on long enough to crank the miniature elevator all the way up to the third floor. They ran into the kitchen. In one movement, Beau cleared the dumbwaiter of the mixing bowls stored there, sending them crashing to the tile floor. He picked up Aubrey and set her bottom on the floor of the tiny car, then helped her to fold herself inside. It was a tight fit, even after he yanked her shoes off and she pulled her knees to her chest and folded her feet under her, and ducked her head. Sara did not protest being squashed between Aubrey's thighs and her rib cage, and Beau did not want to think about what that meant.

He kissed Aubrey quickly on her cheek, which was as close to her mouth as he could get. "See you in a minute. I love you." And he started cranking the elevator upward.

AUBREY TRIED TO KEEP her claustrophobia at bay as the car rose slowly through the dark shaft, breaking up cobwebs as she went. It was musty from many years of disuse, but she thought the air smelled less of the gas, especially as they rose higher.

"We're going to make it, baby," she cooed, more to comfort herself than Sara. "Your uncle Beau loves me. We have to make it through this so we can find out what he intends to do about that.''

The baby's silence terrified her. Her tiny respiratory system probably couldn't withstand as much of the deadly methane as an adult's. Maybe she should have left the baby with Wayne instead of subjecting her—

Aubrey's thoughts froze. Her speed of ascent was slowing. She'd just passed the door to the second floor, where light bled through the cracks of the long-disused door in Wayne's bedroom.

The dumbwaiter stopped.

"Beau!" she screamed. "What's happening?" But she knew. He was being overcome by the gas. "Beau, answer me!"

The car started moving again. With agonizing slowness, it inched its way upward, the progress jerky. She wanted to yell at Beau to give up, to save himself. Maybe he could break through the door to Beronica's quarters. He could shoot through it with his gun.

Please, she prayed. *A couple more feet.* Inches left to go.

"That's it!" she called out. "Stop. Now get the hell out of there!" At first she didn't know how she was going to open the dumbwaiter door on the third floor. Her hands were pinned at her sides. But she managed to work one hand loose. The door, she recalled, opened easily from the inside. She worked her fingers under the rotting wood and jerked it up. Like everything else about the dumbwaiter, it was stiff from disuse—but thankfully not locked. A couple more heaves, and the door was open far enough that Aubrey could roll out onto the floor.

Ignoring her cramped muscles, she stood quickly, hugging the baby to her. The air was definitely fresher up here. She drank in great gulps of it, then listened to see if Sara was breathing. She was—though barely.

No time for CPR. She ran across the small combination living-dining area to the apartment's main door, turned the dead bolt—not a double-keyed one this time, thank God—and flung open the door.

A wave of methane hit her. Beau was there with Wayne, trying to help him up the stairs. "Beau, thank God you're all right! I thought—"

She stopped. Wayne was unconscious. And Beau was staggering.

Beau looked up at Aubrey. "Go. We're right behind you."

She was torn, wanting to help with Wayne. But Sara was already unconscious.

"Go, damn it!" Beau yelled. "We'll make it."

She turned and ran for the fire escape door, off the kitchen.

But when she opened it, she discovered there was no fire escape, as she remembered. This part of the house had apparently been renovated. Now there was just a balcony. She had a view of the driveway where it came around the house to the garage. And David— what was he doing? He'd driven his car around here. Now he sat in it with the top down and he was holding—

The garage door opener. Oh, God. He intended to ignite the house with the press of a button.

Getting to the balcony wouldn't save any of them. They had to get away from the house.

"Beau, hurry!" she called as loudly as she dared. A huge tree grew near the balcony. If she had both her hands free, Aubrey could leap to it. But she had Sara. And Beau would have no hope of saving Wayne.

She tried not to think about that as she hooked her arm through the strap of Sara's little overalls, dangling the baby from her arm like a purse. She couldn't wait another moment. She climbed up on the balcony ledge, sent up a silent prayer, and leaped. Maybe she could sneak up on David and stop him from pushing that button.

She nearly slipped off the branch, but she managed to grab on to another branch and balance herself. A tomboy in her youth, she had no trouble scampering down the tree like a monkey, though she had to be careful not to let Sara bump the tree trunk or get scraped.

She glanced up at the balcony. No sign of Beau. And she couldn't risk calling out now. David would hear her.

She set Sara on the ground behind the tree trunk, then sprinted toward David, moving from shrub to shrub. But his attention was so focused on the house, he never even glanced her way.

But he was still fifty feet away when he lifted his arm and, with an expression of pure, naked hatred, he pushed the button.

The house exploded with a deafening roar, sending a wall of heat that knocked Aubrey off her feet.

"No!" she screamed. But David didn't hear her. He was in his car, heading down the driveway, intent on making his escape before the fire trucks arrived.

He roared past her, never seeing her.

One of the trees near the burning house had caught fire. David had to drive under it. Just as he did, a huge limb from the burning tree dropped directly onto the red Porsche. Aubrey watched in horror as the car careened wildly for a few seconds, then burst into flames itself.

Aubrey turned her face away. And then she was overcome by a wave of dizziness. The ground rushed up to meet them and the world went black.

Chapter Sixteen

Aubrey woke up lying on the grass, the smell of smoke thick in her nose even as she breathed oxygen through a mask. A chubby blond paramedic, whose name tag identified her as Ellen Riggs, was taking her blood pressure. Aubrey blinked her eyes a couple of times.

"You back with us?" Ellen Riggs said, her voice edged with concern.

Aubrey tried to sit up. Her mind felt full of sludge. Then, suddenly, one thought predominated. She grabbed the other woman's arm. "Sara. The baby. Did you find a baby?"

"Your baby is fine. One of the firefighters found her crawling under some bushes. Not a scratch on her."

"But the gas—she breathed in too much methane. She was unconscious!"

"She's okay now. Really."

"What about my uncle? And—oh, my God, Beau. There were two men inside the house when it blew!"

"There was a man in a car…." Ellen said, her face clouded with confusion.

"No, not him. Two others."

"I don't know about any others. They're still fighting the fire."

Aubrey sat up despite Ellen's attempts to calm her down. She ripped the oxygen mask off. "I'm okay now. I have to tell them. I have to let them know to search for Beau and Wayne." She pushed herself to her knees, then her feet. Her legs felt rubbery, but after a few false steps they supported her.

She'd been lying on the grass, some distance from the house. There were fire trucks everywhere, police cars, and dozens of bystanders just watching. A TV news van was just pulling in the driveway.

How long since the explosion? Aubrey wondered frantically.

She searched until she saw someone she knew—Craig. And he was holding Sara! Aubrey rushed up to him and grabbed them in a bear hug. "Thanks for bringing in the cavalry."

"A little slow. I'm sorry, Aubrey. By the time I rounded up some uniforms, explained everything, and got over here, I was too late." And there was such a profound look of grief on his face that he didn't have to tell Aubrey the worst part.

"You didn't find Beau? Or my uncle?"

"They were inside the house, then." It sounded as if Aubrey had just confirmed his worst fears.

She nodded. "On the third floor, or the stairs leading up to it. They might be all right. Look, some of the house is still standing...."

Craig handed the baby to her, then put his arm around her shoulders. "Stay here. I'm going to go tell them." He started to walk away, then stopped and turned back. "Who was in the car?"

"David." She grimaced, then swallowed back the

very real lump of grief in her throat—grief for the cousin she remembered, not the desperate, cold-blooded killer he'd become. "I saw what happened to him."

Looking grim, Craig turned again and continued with his mission. But as he neared the house, a commotion started somewhere inside the house, or what was left of it. She heard a lot of shouting. Then two firemen appeared carrying a person who was frighteningly still. Aubrey recognized the blue pajamas, looking oddly pristine. No burns or black smoke marks, which made her hopeful.

Ellen, the blond paramedic, took off like a shot toward Aubrey's uncle. But Aubrey felt as if she were rooted to the driveway. She watched and waited…and waited.

And then, amazingly, she saw a man walking out of the fire. She held her breath, afraid to hope, afraid she was hallucinating. He wasn't wearing a black-and-yellow fireman's protective clothing. He had on black jeans and a black T-shirt and motorcycle boots. Blood streamed over his face, but he was upright, walking more or less under his own power, though he leaned heavily on one of the firefighters as the other man escorted him out of the burning house.

She knew she should stay back, out of the way, but she couldn't stand there any longer. She broke into a run and didn't stop until she reached him, skidding to a halt only when she realized that throwing her arms around him might knock him to the ground.

"Beau?"

He glanced up and saw her. His eyes shone with wonder. "You're all right."

"Yes, I'm fine. Sara's fine. You're not, though, you're hurt." She realized then he was soaking wet.

Beau dismissed the fireman. "I'm okay, thanks. Thank you." The fireman returned to his duties, and Beau walked as far as the fountain, then dropped onto one of the stone benches. It was where they'd sat that night after the gas leak, when they'd made up after their argument—then promptly argued again.

Her fault, Aubrey silently acknowledged.

Ellen reappeared and quietly started mopping the blood off Beau's face. She seemed to know enough not to intrude.

"You got soaked by the fire hoses," Aubrey said, unable to think of anything else to say. The shock of the explosion had turned her thoughts to molasses.

"Not the hoses," Beau said. "The explosion blew us free, clear into the swimming pool. It was the only thing that saved me. I had hold of Wayne. I tried to save him, Aubrey. Really."

"I know you did." She grabbed one of his bloodied hands and brought it up to her cheek. "That was the most selfless thing I've ever seen anybody do. You could have saved yourself, but you stayed behind to help him."

He shook his head. His voice was thick with emotion. "I don't think I succeeded."

Ellen shook her head. "He was gone when I got to him. We would have worked on him longer, but he was wearing a DNR bracelet."

"Do Not Resuscitate," Beau clarified, though Aubrey already knew what it was. "Damn."

Ellen handed Beau some gauze. "It's just a small cut, on your forehead there. I think if you put pressure on it the bleeding will stop and you won't need stitches.''

He took the gauze. Ellen gave Aubrey's shoulder a final, sympathetic squeeze before leaving them.

''Please don't blame yourself for Wayne's death, Beau. You did everything you could. And he was dying anyway. Mary, his hospice nurse, said he only had a few hours left.''

They were silent for a few moments. The only one who made any noise was Sara, who had no clue what was going on and seemed to enjoy all the color and excitement swirling around her. She showed no ill effects from the gas.

''What about David?'' Beau asked.

Aubrey pointed at the smoldering hunk of twisted metal that had once been a beautiful sports car. ''He didn't make it.''

''I'm sorry. I can't think of anything else to say.''

''I'm sorry he tried to destroy so many lives, including his own,'' she said. ''He touched off the gas with the garage door opener. I saw him do it, right before he…he…'' She couldn't go on.

Beau slipped his arm around her. ''It'll be all right, Aubrey. I know you've lost a lot. But you've got Sara. And you've got me.''

''Do I?''

''Forever. Eternally. Whether you want me or not. Maybe it took me a while to come to my senses, but when I realized you might still be in danger, it was like someone flipped a switch inside my head—inside my heart. I realized I was crazy in love with you.''

''But I was so horrible to you.''

''You love your brother, that's all. And you can't reconcile the brother you know with the facts I laid out. Maybe you'll never reconcile them, but that's something we'll have to work around.''

She pulled away and looked at him. He'd forgotten to keep the gauze pressed against his cut, and it was still oozing blood. She took the gauze and did it for him, wishing she could tend to his other wounds—the emotional wounds she inflicted with her cruel words—as easily. ''We don't have to work around it. I believe you, Beau, as I should have all along. Gavin was desperate. Of course you wouldn't have shot him unless you had to. No man who could behave so selflessly, risking your own life trying to save a dying old man, would have shot his best friend for money. That's not who you are. I should have seen it before. I knew you, Beau. I've loved you a long time. I just forgot who you are for a while.''

He hugged her to him, including Sara in his embrace. ''That's all I've ever wanted from you. If I died tomorrow I'd die happy.''

''You're not going to die tomorrow, or any time soon. Don't even talk about it. I won't let you. No one else I love is going to die. That stops here and now.''

''Agreed, honey. If you promise to love me, I promise not to die. Not till I'm a hundred, at least.''

They sat entwined, the three of them, and numbly watched the firefighters extinguish the blaze. The house was a total loss. The paintings, the antique furniture, all gone, destroyed as thoroughly as the Clarendon family. But just as Beau had emerged, injured but still vital, from the flames and soot, Aubrey knew something good had come of the tragedy. She and Beau had found their way to each other. And they would start over, a new family, like a phoenix rising from the ashes.

AT DAWN on a Saturday in late August, two months after the explosion, Beau and Aubrey were married in a simple ceremony in the rose garden behind the mayor's house. Beau had wanted to elope to Las Vegas, but Aubrey had nixed that idea. "You just don't want to wear a tie," she'd said. "Besides, I want to wait until after Gavin's parole hearing. It would be so nice to have him at my wedding."

Beau had agreed. Then he'd moved heaven and earth to make sure Gavin made parole. He'd made sure everyone on that board was convinced that Gavin was a different man from the one who'd committed the crime. Or rather, that he was once again the man who'd been Beau's best friend, before his addiction. He and Gavin's lawyer had rounded up everyone associated with the addiction program Gavin had successfully completed, all of whom testified about how earnest Gavin had been, how badly he'd wanted to kick his habit, how hard he'd worked, how faithfully he'd attended the meetings.

Aubrey had cried with joy when Gavin had been granted parole. But her joy had quickly turned to bewilderment when Gavin had almost immediately withdrawn from all contact with her. He'd made his appointments with his parole officer, but he'd refused to talk to Aubrey.

"I'm not going to let it bother me," Aubrey had declared to anyone who expressed concern about the situation. "He'll come around when he's ready. Maybe after two years of living in such close quarters with so many people, he just needs some time alone."

Of course, Aubrey would assign the most innocent explanation to Gavin's behavior, Beau thought. That was Aubrey. Beau didn't want to point out that Gavin was probably staying away because of him.

He put that out of his mind the morning of the wedding. It was a comfortable seventy degrees as he drove his Mustang through the darkness, his last few minutes as a single man. He was marrying Aubrey, and nothing was going to dim his happiness.

She was an incredibly beautiful bride in her grandmother's satin gown. As they stood before the minister, a slight breeze played with Aubrey's lace veil. The sun rose over the horizon and peeked through the trunks of the surrounding trees, dappling her face as they exchanged vows. And as they kissed, one blindingly bright ray of sunlight found them, illuminating them in a natural spotlight as if the heavens were granting their approval of the union.

Though the hour was ridiculously early, they'd managed to assemble a small group of well-wishers to witness the event. All of the First Strike bounty hunters were there. Some of Aubrey's fellow professors and teaching assistants from the University had made it. Her parents, of course. Beau didn't really have any family to invite, but that was something he'd gotten over a long time ago. He was more than happy to let Aubrey's family adopt him.

Mary, the hospice nurse who'd cared for Wayne, had come, too. She said that in her line of work she attended more funerals than she liked, so the wedding of a family member she'd grown close to was a real treat.

Then there was Sara, who had the nerve to sleep through the whole thing. Which was probably better than squalling.

After the brief ceremony, everyone moved to a large

pavilion for the usual stuff—a fluffy white wedding cake, a sinful chocolate groom's cake, this one in the shape of a Mustang. There was champagne and orange juice, and lots of toasts to future happiness. Beau took a lot of ribbing for his dove gray morning suit—complete with white tie—which Aubrey had shoehorned him into. But he'd have done anything to please her, because he felt privileged to be her husband. Just lucky as hell.

"So, you're gonna do the daddy thing." It was Lori, who was taking her turn holding Sara. Sara had awakened, and she was being unusually cheerful, charming everyone silly.

"Something like that," Beau said, taking the baby from Lori and holding her with an ease he wouldn't have imagined a couple of months ago. But he'd had a lot of practice the past few weeks, and he'd decided a baby girl was a *lot* better than a puppy. "Sara's father decided she would be better off with us, though he'll still be a part of her life." Beau nuzzled the baby. "I'm gonna teach her how to play ball, and work on cars, and how to say no to all the boys. Ain't that right, sweetpea?" He rubbed his nose against hers in an Eskimo kiss.

Lori's mouth dropped open. "Oh, my gosh. I've never seen you with a baby."

"And I've never seen your legs," he said pointedly, glancing down at the appendages in question peeking out from her blue sleeveless dress. "Gawd, you even have nail polish on your toes. Pink."

"I wear dresses," she said defensively. "Just not to work. Ace would never let me do anything fun if I dressed like a girl." She wrinkled her nose.

"Did I hear my name taken in vain?" Ace joined

them, looking almost dapper in neatly creased trousers, pinstriped shirt, and sober blue silk tie. He was on his third or fourth champagne cocktail and feeling no pain. He put an arm around Lori's shoulders. "You look so…so cute!"

Lori stuck her tongue out at him. "I *hate* that word. I am not cute. Bounty hunters are not cute."

"Aw, I dunno," Rex chimed in, unable to resist a good opportunity to tease Beau. He'd donned his least worn pair of jeans and a T-shirt without any off-color slogans. "Maddox here looks pretty cute holding a baby."

Beau was formulating a smart comeback, but someone approaching the pavilion caught his attention. He tensed, all his well-honed instincts coming into play. Though Aubrey's enemies were no longer a threat, there were plenty of people walking around free who didn't like him.

But his tension melted when he recognized the determined jut of the chin, and that brisk, no-nonsense walk, now with a slight limp.

Gavin Schuyler.

A different sort of apprehension speared Beau's gut. Despite Gavin's recent behavior, Beau knew his former friend loved his sister and would do nothing to hurt her. But Gavin didn't necessarily feel the same about Beau. The fact Beau had been instrumental in Gavin's release didn't really make up for the fact he'd shot Gavin.

Aubrey, who'd been busy dancing with every male in the place as Motown tunes poured out of a boom box, now returned to Beau's side. She grasped his arm and squeezed until she just about cut off his circulation, and it was clear she saw what he did.

"Is that…it is!" She released Beau's arm and ran down the walkway to meet her brother.

Beau watched as they embraced. Several other people had noted the new arrival, and conversation grew hushed.

"Who is that?" Lori asked.

Beau answered her. "Gavin Schuyler."

Lori gasped again. "The one you shot?" Then she clamped her hand over her mouth. "Sorry. That was tactless."

"But it's the truth." Beau had been positive he and Aubrey, with their newfound trust and mutual understanding, could breeze through anything about Gavin that came up. But seeing him here, at their wedding of all places, still thin and pale from prison, gave him a moment of unease.

Then Aubrey dragged her brother into their midst. "Everyone, look who's here!" she announced, as if news of his arrival hadn't already spread through the small group like a brushfire. A moment of awkward silence followed her words. Then everyone was talking at once, and people were hugging Gavin and shaking his hand as if he were a returning hero instead of an ex-con.

For that, Beau was very, very grateful.

Then all at once he was standing face-to-face with Gavin, the first time he'd seen him since the parole hearing, when they didn't talk to each other directly. And Beau didn't know what to say. At least he was still holding the baby. Surely Gavin wouldn't deck a man holding a baby.

Gavin looked at Beau, then Sara, then Aubrey. "Is this my new little cousin? Or is she my niece? I'm a little confused."

"You and me both," Aubrey said. "Gavin, this is Sara. I guess she'll be your niece as soon as we adopt her. You want to hold her?"

"Uh—"

Aubrey grabbed Sara from Beau and unceremoniously dumped the baby into Gavin's arms. He took Sara, and Sara looked up at him and smiled her angelic smile and said, "Ga-ga."

Gavin's face lit up with a smile. "She already knows my name."

Beau didn't have the heart to tell him Sara called everyone and everything ga-ga. Instead, he rejoiced in the fact that Sara's innocence could be a guiding force in healing the hurts for Gavin—as she'd been for himself and Aubrey. She'd been through a lot already in her young life, and yet she smiled, because she didn't even realize she should do otherwise.

He'd do anything he could to make sure she stayed that way.

Gavin looked up at Beau. "Hey."

"Hey yourself."

Aubrey linked arms with both of them and beamed her own angelic smile.

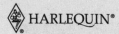

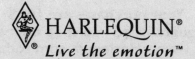

If you enjoyed what you just read,
then we've got an offer you can't resist!

Take 2 bestselling
love stories FREE!

Plus get a FREE surprise gift!

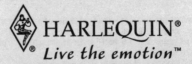

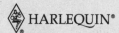

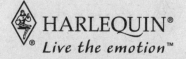

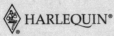

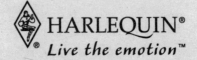